The Cassandra Curse

• • • • • • • • • • •

Should've gone for something easier, like the Sleeping Beauty Curse....

(100 years of sleep sounds nice right now)

Hope Bolinger

CHICKEN SCRATCH BOOKS

WWW.CHICKENSCRATCHBOOKS.COM

Chicken Scratch Books

PO Box 104

Wisdom, MT 59761

www.chickenscratchbooks.com

Publisher's Note: This is a work of fiction. Names, characters, places, and incidents are a product of the author's imagination. Locales and public names are sometimes used for atmospheric purposes. Any resemblance to actual people, living or dead, or to businesses, companies, events, institutions, or locales is completely coincidental.

Ordering Information: Special discounts are available on quantity purchases by corporations, associations, and others. For details, contact the publisher at the address above.

First Chicken Scratch Books Printing, 2021

ISBN 978-1-953743-10-7 (paperback)

ISBN 978-1-953743-11-4 (ebook)

Printed in the United States of America

To Dad, who told me weird stories at night where the main characters died or something wonky happened. This is all your fault.

And to eighth grade me who would've worn a tutu if her school didn't have strict dress code guidelines. Thanks to you, I wear tutus now. I hope you're happy.

Chapter 1

Should've Worn the T-Rex Costume Instead. . . .

Charity applied the last bit of white clown makeup to her face. Today she would make the world a better place.

She stared at the mirror that hung from her bedroom door. A face with large red-painted lips and sheet white skin stared back. The red hair was hers. Courtesy of her parent's genes, she already came with part clown attached to her.

Her chest froze for a moment. Would her peers laugh when they saw her?

She shook the feelings away. Probably, but that didn't matter. Today was her classmate Willow's birthday, and she would make it special. Willow liked clowns, right? She kept getting all her fellow students from Almsgiving Middle School mixed up.

A buzzing rumbled on her bed. Her iPad sent shock-waves up and down her unicorn comforter. Beside the device, her neon green stuffed squid Inkheart jolted because of the incoming call from . . . Io. Her best friend.

Charity grinned. She swiped the green button and held

up the screen to her face so Io could catch her in her full clown glory.

Io, whose frizzy black hair took up most of the upper part of the screen, squinted at the camera. "Do I even want to know?"

"Willow's birthday." She hoped it was enough of an explanation. Judging by the way that Io's dark eyelids closed over her brown irises more, it wasn't.

But then her friend shrugged and tugged a quilt closer to her chest. "Anyway, you left your Ancient History textbook at my house on Saturday. You want me to give it to you at lunch?"

Of course I forgot my homework at her house again. Stupid, Charity.

Charity tucked her hair behind her ear and untucked it again. Ever since *the incident* three years back, she'd lost her smarts and traded them for dumbs.

"Yes, please." School had a nasty habit, this eighth-grade year, of placing Charity in the opposite classes of her best friends. She only shared lunch with Io, and art with her other best friend Stefan. "Where'd you get that quilt?"

Io nuzzled her nose on a blue star-shaped pattern in the fabric. "Dad's out of town for a long business trip in China. I'm staying with my grandma for a while."

Huh, he must've left on Sunday, after their sleepover. In the three years she'd known Io, Charity had only seen the man a few times. He spent most of his days in a cubicle.

"Anyway." Io dropped the quilt and tore her fingers

through some wayward fizzy curls. "Grandma likes to get to places early. So I should probably go before she yells at me to get downstairs again. See you at lunch."

Before Charity could wave, the screen went dark. She glanced up at her door and found her mother gray-faced and leaning against the frame. Ever since this summer her mom had taken a lot more naps and struggled to hold herself in an upright position.

"Come on, kiddo." Her mom shielded a yawn behind her palm. "Time for school." She turned to the hallway and then halted. "Do I want to know about the clown costume?"

"Probably." Charity grabbed her backpack off her bed and looped the straps around her shoulders. They bounded down the stairs and into the car.

The trip to the school was colorful as always. Almsgiving, the town she'd lived in since second grade, boasted every hue imaginable. The book shop downtown still had a large human-sized spider on the awning left over from Halloween. A popcorn store, that always smelled of cheese and caramel from their car, had repainted their storefront again. This time they went for neon pink and green stripes. Even her favorite ice cream shop, The Scoop, had planted a large new ceramic cone out front, complete with a cherry and "hot fudge" that reached the sidewalk.

Even if Charity couldn't blend in with her classmates at Almsgiving Middle, she could feel right at home in these streets.

She couldn't tell when the paradigm shift happened. It

was, like, fifth grade = cool, you have a dinosaur onesie?

Sixth grade = umm, why do you have a dinosaur onesie?

Seventh grade = Charity, you need to burn that dinosaur onesie.

Clearly, their school needed to address their arsonist program.

Speaking of school, they'd arrived at the yellowed sign for Almsgiving Middle School. Mom, who said nothing the whole car ride, pulled into a snaking line of cars. At last, they reached the entrance, and Charity bounded out of the car.

She ignored the sniggers of a girl and boy who held hands when they walked past.

She waved at her mom who threw up a hand before the car coasted out of the parking lot. Then Charity followed the couple inside and almost bumped into a sixth-grader in pigtails who hugged a stuffed bear under her chin. Once Charity stumbled into the front glass doors—stupid clown shoes— she almost collided with an eighth-grader who had already sprouted some whiskers under his chin.

"Sorry," she skirted past him. Her eyes grew wide when she spotted the clock in the hallway. She'd had to wake up Mom this morning, so they had a far slower start than usual. Now she had two minutes before the school day began.

She waddled down the hallway and past the sea of bodies that weaved between lockers. Students, when they noticed her costume, both giggled into their fists and jumped out of the way, to avoid the large shoes from tripping them. At last, she'd reached the room at the end of the hallway with 134 on the door frame.

Charity tripped on her clown shoes at the homeroom entrance.

They wedged inside the blue classroom door like a doorstop. Giggles erupted from the front seat of the classroom, and in her periphery, she spotted someone in a pink long sleeve pointing at her.

Well, that's not kind. Pointing.

She grimaced and yanked her shoe out . . . proceeding to bonk her forehead on the edge of the door. White clown paint smeared all over the blue.

What a great way to start off today. But it'll be all worth it when Willow sees this costume.

Since her almost-friend Willow couldn't go to the circus field trip last year, Charity figured she could bring the circus to her on her birthday.

Then, and finally then, I'll make today a better place.

The mission she'd sought to do since three years ago. All had gone according to plan . . . until this past summer.

She held a hand to her forehead and scanned the classroom. Even though white makeup covered her cheeks, she could still feel her face grow red when another soft giggle sounded from the front row.

No, stop it emotions. Stop feeling. You're doing this for Willow's birthday.

She dug her nails into her palms.

A girl with ramen noodle curly hair and mascara wrinkled her nose at Charity. "What are you wearing?" The girl gestured to Charity's polka dot outfit.

Charity tried to force a grin at her before realizing, two seconds later, that she'd already painted a red smile on her face earlier. She let her lips fade into a thin line. Charity forced her head toward the linoleum floor to try and avoid the million eyes that seemed to sear into her forehead. Didn't help that the clown costume packed about two million degrees.

The ramen-noodle hair girl tapped her shimmery boots in a rhythmic pattern. "Charity, I asked you a question."

Charity bit her lip. "Have you seen Willow anywhere?" She scanned the feet in the classroom for Willow's signature blue shoes.

"I think I saw her by her locker."

"You did?" Hope leaped into Charity's throat, but her neck got caught in the ruffle on her clown costume. She lifted her chin. "I heard it was her birthday, and I figured since she couldn't go to the circus with us last year, I wanted to do something nice . . . ." When she met the girl's eyes, she realized they were narrowed.

"You *do* realize she has Coulrophobia, right? Is this, like, a late Halloween prank or something?"

Coulro-what? Is that some kind of disease?

"Is she going to die or something? That sounds awfully contagious."

The girl with the ramen hair pinched her nose. "It's a wonder you're in normal-people classes, Charity. You're really slow sometimes."

This comment flamed Charity's cheeks.

10

Footsteps echoed behind her and died at the sound of the bell. Charity turned around and almost tripped Willow with her shoes. Thank goodness, Charity jumped back just in time, but Willow still collapsed on the floor.

At first, Charity thought Willow was cackling from the sight of her in the clown costume.

At last! It was worth it after all.

But moments later she recognized the howl coming from Willow. She wasn't laughing . . . she was crying.

And then . . . Willow couldn't stop shaking.

Charity's eyes went wide, and she found her oxygen didn't filter all that well through the red felt nose.

Oh no, what did I do?

It appeared Willow had a hard time breathing, too, because her breaths came out short and ragged. She'd covered her ears with her palms.

Charity trembled right along with her until the teacher materialized beside Willow. He glared at Charity and then reached into his pocket to pull out a packet of pink sheets. With a red pen, he scrawled on one and tore it off the pad. The top of the sheet read, "Vice Principal's Office."

What did I do?

Chapter 2

Would've Created a Collage from Detention Slips. . . .

Charity's clown shoes kicked back and forth under the hard seat. Why did the vice-principal have to paint his office all gray? It reminded her of gravestones.

She didn't meet his eyes.

"I killed her, didn't I?" Charity rubbed the heel of her palm up her cheek to block the stream of tears. She glanced at her hand. It had white face paint smudged on the pink skin. Just like it had on the door back in homeroom. "Mom says I kill everyone with kindness."

She frowned at the floor and tried to block out the echoing voice of the ramen-noodle girl. *"It's a wonder you're in normal people classes, Charity."*

I'm smart. I am.

Her belly shook from holding in tears.

It's just like I'm speaking Greek or something, and we don't understand each other's languages.

Vice Principal Rancor cleared his throat and glanced at the gray clock hanging above the door of his office before steepling his fingers together. He banged them against the desk. "Charity, Coulrophobia isn't a disease. It's a fear of clowns."

Charity stopped mid-sniffle and bunched her nostrils.

Wowser, Rancor likes the smell of lemon fresh spray in his office, doesn't he?

She reached up to plug her nose but thought better of it. He might get insulted if she complained about his preferred office scent.

"F-fear of clowns?"

"A rather acute one." Rancor straightened himself in his chair, and if possible, made himself even more towering. Then he narrowed his dark, birdlike eyes. "You saw the beginnings of the panic attack before Mr. Corin sent you here, yes?"

"Yes, sir, but all the same, I do have a funeral speech prepared for all the classmates in case something goes horribly wrong."

Principal Rancor was busy typing something on the computer and didn't appear to hear the last part.

With me, something 'horribly wrong' is bound to happen. Such a shame to go at only thirteen years old.

Charity squeezed her eyes shut, then opened them. She scrunched her eyebrows as visions from the locker room flooded her mind from the other day, when she'd read Willow her 'funeral speech.'

"Umm, why did you write a speech for when I die?" Willow asked this while tying her basketball shoe laces.

"Oh, I did it for everyone in study hall. I hope to have one for everyone in the class. Two hundred students, and statistics are abysmal you know. Who knows if we'll all make it to our twenties?"

Willow didn't pass her the basketball during practice.

In complete honesty, ever since Charity turned thirteen this past August disastrous omens seemed to follow her, hence the need to create funeral speeches. When she held open the front door to the school for her almost-friend Xochil the other day, Xochil tripped on a puddle. And her almost-acquaintance Robert face-planted into an open locker door when she offered to carry some of his books for him the other day.

Principal Rancor cleared his throat again. "Miss Charity, I'd been certain you'd have known of Miss Willow's fear of clowns when she stayed home during the class field trip to the circus up in Cleveland last year."

Huh.

I thought Willow's mom made her stay home from that because she couldn't afford to go.

Hence the clown costume. Maybe since she couldn't go to the circus, she could bring the show to her.

Charity sank into her chair in the office and watched the starfish-shaped fan on the ceiling whirl round and round.

"I'm certain you have an excellent explanation for why you not only broke the school dress code but left Willow to cry in the sick room after giving her a panic attack."

A sniffle from the nurse's office a few doors down broke the silence.

Probably Willow. Or that poor secretary, Mr. Morrow.

He cried all the time. When once asked why he teared up like he'd cut an onion, during her last visit to the office, he claimed he had something called "PBA."

Not a clue what peanut butter (PB) and apple (A) sandwiches have to do with tears. Maybe he's got a short lunch break. Bosses can be unkind like that and not give people time to eat.

"Miss Charity, I asked a question."

Slow as always, even in her replies.

Maybe that ramen-noodle girl had a point.

"Birthday," Charity mumbled, her feet mirroring the fan above her. Two big maroon clown shoes whirled round and round. "Willow's birthday."

Rancor quirked an eyebrow, reminding Charity of a fuzzy caterpillar that crawled on the trees in her backyard. He hunched forward, a miracle for that stiff spine, and tapped away at his keyboard.

Moments later, he uncoiled.

"It says here that her birthday isn't until March, four months from now."

"Darn. Must've mixed up her birthday with Elm." Tree names, how typical.

The Vice Principal's lips pressed together until they formed an emoji-thin line. "Miss Charity this isn't the first instance of you entering my office at the expense of another classmate."

No siree, thanks to her PB (hold the A) bars she brought Oliver for his thirteenth birthday last year. She baked them instead of studying for her Life Science test because his mom worked retail and didn't have time to bring in a treat for homeroom.

Turned out, he had a peanut allergy. And not just a, oh no (shudder) peanuts are my weakness allergy, but a Boss Battle Can't Be In The Same Room As Peanuts Or I'll Get Anaphylactic Shock allergy.

And also turned out, the teacher had mentioned the allergy at the same time Charity had landed herself in the Vice Principal's office for putting a taxidermy bunny on Ava's desk. She guessed later when Ava mentioned she liked "stuffed animals" that didn't mean *dead stuffed animals.*

Whoops. She swallowed, throat catching on the purple ruffle of her clown outfit.

"I'm sorry, Mr. Rancor. Really, I am. I do mean well. Every one of the things you've called me in here for had the best of intentions. I just want to make the world a better place."

Rancor sighed and pinched the bridge of his nose, right between his caterpillar eyebrows. "Charity, I know you meant well . . . but, it feels like every time you try to kill someone with kindness, you might actually *kill* them." Another sigh. "If I have to call you in here again, we'll have to explore other methods of punishment aside from a detention."

He slid open his drawer and tore off a pink sheet of

paper from a legal pad.

The pink slip almost caught on her felt red nose. Her eyes crossed as she read "DETENTION" in faded black letters.

"Wash your face and ask Mr. Morrow to peek into the lost and found bin. There will surely be some clothes in your . . . size." He hesitated before the last word. Charity wasn't exactly a skinny minny.

But that means I give the best hugs.

Not that anyone would accept her offer for free hugs.

She scooted her chair back and jumped out, only to lurch into the desk, knocking over a glass apple with "#1 Vice Principal" engraved in white. Stupid clown shoes.

Rancor puffed a sigh. "And please don't let me see you in here again, unless I'm congratulating you for getting straight A's this quarter."

Straight-C average. Oh yeah, he'd never see her in here again.

Ramen noodle girl could be right. Maybe I shouldn't be in normal people classes.

She dug her nails into her palms. Her cheeks burned so much that she bet she could heat up her aunt's creamed corn casserole on them.

She shuffled out of the office and flinched when the bang of the door sent wind down her polka dot outfit. Right foot, left foot.

Oh, whoops now we're tripping and catching balance on the right foot.

She caught herself on the front desk before she

face-planted into a succulent plant stationed by a stack of field trip forms for the school's band.

"Hi, Mr. Morrow. I'd love to go shopping. Got anything nice in that bin of yours?"

Mr. Morrow swiped a Kleenex on his scraggly mustache, catching a tear, before reaching down and placing the lost and found bin on the counter. Charity hoisted herself on her tiptoes and almost fell right in.

Shoot, no shoes in here.

Ah well, she dug out a boy's hoodie and some gym shorts.

These'll have to do.

After all, Rancor outlawed sports jerseys in the dress code, too.

"Thanks, Mr. Morrow!" She stumbled again and flung onto the counter, fingers barely hanging on. "Wow, don't think I've been this uncoordinated since our class went roller skating."

Morrow squinched his eyelids and glanced at the hallway, barricading tears. "It's a far walk to the girl's restroom."

"'S fine. I'll just pop these bad boys off." She pulled herself up and tried nudging off one shoe with the toe cap of another.

Oh, well, that didn't work.

Morrow's smile disappeared in his black beard. "Tell you what, Charity. Go ahead and use the staff restroom to change." He jabbed his thumb over his shoulder at a wooden door. "So your classmates don't have to see you like . . . ."

He broke off into tears.

Someone get this poor man a peanut butter and apple sandwich.

Charity waddled to the bathroom entrance and clicked open the metal latch. Clinging to the sink for dear life, she shut the door and the lights and fan hummed to life. She straddled the toilet seat to pop off the clown shoes and changed into the new outfit.

Now, for the clown makeup.

One paper towel, two paper towels, ten paper towels later she succeeded in wiping off the white and red streaks of paint. Well, at least a now very pink face justified the killing of all these trees. "If you ask me, the *kind* thing to do would be to let me just wear all this makeup for the rest of the day and save the environment."

Then again all her good intentions landed her in here. Was any other middle schooler this cursed?

The only other person she could think of who had as much bad luck as her this year was Io. At least, from what she could tell at lunch, Io had indicated most of the soccer players on her team had unfriended her, or at least, kept their distance.

"I usually like to pass other people the ball during games, so they have a chance to shoot." Io had said this over a bite of a cafeteria burger last Wednesday. "But every time I do that, the other team manages to steal the ball. I don't know what happened to me and soccer, but Coach won't play me anymore."

Charity picked up the pink slip she'd left on the toilet

seat to tuck the paper into her green Bowser backpack. It was green, like the character's from the Mario video games, complete with white fabric spikes.

Wait a second, did Mr. Rancor write her a note on the back? And when did he ever use a *purple* pen?

She squinted in the dim bathroom lighting to make out the words.

Charity,

Since you turned thirteen, have you noticed that you can't seem to do anything right? That all of your actions end in disaster? Want to stop the curse?

Meet us at Lake Prespa by the school on Saturday at 9 a.m. sharp.

-- The Cassandra Coalition

Chapter 3

Would've Preferred the School's Origami Club, But Okay. . . .

And that's how you make an origami swan."

Charity stared at her snowball made out of the paper in the art teacher's classroom.

Eh, close enough.

A giggle stung her ears and she swiveled around to watch Elm pull back the finger she'd pointed in Charity's direction.

Again, with the pointing! Rude!

Willow, next to her, turned scarlet and she hunched over the green paper swan she'd made: all the edges formed perfect angles.

Heat lit in Charity's cheeks and she spun around to see if she could try again. But Miss Tegea had already put away the square sheets of paper into a bin clear across the classroom.

She hunched into her shoulders and hoped that she could turn into a turtle and disappear.

Something jabbed into her side, an elbow. Its owner, Stefan, withdrew his arm and nodded at her disaster of a swan.

"You made an ugly duckling, Chair."

She opened her mouth to say, "You're one to talk," but stopped herself.

Stefan had sprouted acne earlier this year and his voice cracked like an egg on every word. Not to mention, he shot up six inches from last year and so none of his clothes fit. He did rock that my-pants-don't-cover-my-ankles look, though.

"Sometimes I like the fairy tales told in reverse, from a swan to an ugly duckling," Charity said.

Her mom reminded her of a swan. Long feathery eyelashes, and an uncanny territorial instinct that could scare away any lake creature, if they had lived on a lake. She'd have to settle with yelling at Mr. Dinklestein, their neighbor, for cutting their grass without asking.

Speaking of lake, this past summer, on Charity's thirteenth birthday, she and her mom *had* visited a lake near the school. Almsgiving liked to throw a town fair at the waterside, water activities, funnel cake fries, and booths for charities included.

The swan came out in her mom when she squawked at a man who tried to steal their canoe they'd brought.

Ever since that day in August, all of Charity's actions ended in disaster. Including this stupid origami 'swan.'

She chewed on her lip and threw her snowball into her backpack.

"We can start over," Stefan suggested. "If you get a new piece of paper, I can show you."

Charity tore off some loose lip skin. The teacher had already put away the extra sheets. She unzipped her bag and dug for a spare page.

Nope, that's the rock I found outside the school earlier with the cool skull shape on it.

Also nope, a dead snake she wanted to give to Reilly, a boy in her Algebra class who said he liked snakes.

Tomorrow, she decided, she would do that. She was still working on his eulogy and could pair the gifts as a two-for-one deal.

At last, she struck paper! Eureka!

Eu-paper-a . . . ah, that's the detention slip.

All the heat from her clown suit from earlier came rushing back until she broke out into a sweat. Laughter from classmates behind her echoed in her ears.

Wonder if Mom would be open to homeschooling me.

Mom had homeschooled her prior to middle school and often remarked about how far ahead Charity had advanced in her schooling for her age. She'd even skipped a grade, hence joining seventh grade at a mere twelve years old when her mom sent Charity to public school so she could work an office job.

"Will this work to make another swan?" Charity showed Stefan the pink sheet of paper.

Stefan frowned and then ran his dark fingers through his dark curly hair. "Don't you need that when you show up to detention?"

"It's a slip, not a ticket to Cedar Point. Rancor probably told the monitor who's gonna show up on Saturday for detention." Besides, the monitor Mr. Giannis knew Charity by now. Nice bald man with a wife who also had a large bald spot.

At least they don't take long showers.

A spurt of air flew out of Stefan's nostrils, and a little boogey. "Fair enough. Now, first you'll want to fold . . . what's this about a curse?"

Oh, right. She'd completely forgotten about the curse thing. She had wanted to bring it up at lunch with Io, but she got distracted when Io described all her grandma's quilts that the woman apparently hoarded in her house.

In either case, Charity *always* felt cursed and didn't quite feel like pursuing the subject at the moment when a paper swan needed to come into being.

"Stefan, I need you to focus."

"And Cassandra. You know there's an Ancient Greek legend about her."

Oh boy, he loves his Percy Jackson books.

"I don't know. Now, swan me."

"And since when does Rancor ever write with a purple pen?"

Charity threw up her arms, knocking back the wooden table at which she was stationed. "At this rate, I'll settle for an origami dog."

A bell sounded behind them. School had ended for the day.

She huffed a sigh and pushed her chair back until her clown shoes were almost fully visible under the table.

"Never mind, I'll YouTube it."

Her Bowser backpack strap clung to her left shoulder as they meandered toward the halls. Classmates of all walks of puberty surrounded them. One couple stared lovingly into each other's eyes to the point where Charity wanted to vomit. Beside them, a girl showed off a popular dance from a video game to a group of friends clustered around her.

Charity waddled, and a squirm released from her gut. At last, she could head to the locker room and put on her shoes for basketball practice.

"Coach is weird about that, not letting us wear our basketball shoes anywhere but the basketball court," she told Stefan in the hallway. Various seventh-graders dodged her shoes.

"I think you should wear the clown shoes for practice." Stefan's lips twitched. "Maybe you can trip the opponents."

"Stefan, you don't know the first thing about basketball. You can't trip anyone. They'd call a foul on you."

"It's a joke, Charity. I'm being sarcastic."

"Oh." She blinked, heat blooming her cheeks. "Sorry, I guess I'm a little slow."

"Besides, I never understood why you did the sport in the first place. It's one of the rudest ones if you ask me."

True, Coach did bench her because she would apologize for fouling other players on the court. Weird thing, during the last game, she tried to keep her arms pin-straight toward the gym ceiling as a player on the opposing team crashed into her for a layup shot.

Even though she tried her best not to touch the player, since hitting someone counted as a foul, the girl ran right into her palm and her nose immediately spouted blood like water fountain sprinklers the school had installed in the body of water nearest to them: Lake Prespa.

The same lake where the town held a festival back in August on Charity's birthday.

"I swear, Stefan, everything I touch dies. Or gets seriously injured. Think I should put on some gloves?"

"Goes against school dress code."

"Well so is wearing a dinosaur onesie, and that didn't stop me."

"Charity . . . Rancor did stop you. Remember? You had to write 'I will not wear a dinosaur onesie or rawr at my classmates as they emerge from the restroom' one hundred times."

Her wrists never recovered from that torture.

"Guess I'll have to chop off my hands then. Seems like the only practical solution."

"You *do* realize you can touch things with other parts of your body, like your feet or elbow," Stefan said.

Back to the drawing board.

Chapter 4

Should've Dropped Out of School and Worked the Runway. . . .

harity," Stefan squinted at her through the screen on the FaceTime app, "are you wearing a tutu?"

"Why yes. Thought we'd go for a change of pace. Clown shoes give your feet blisters."

"Right but—" He sucked in his bottom lip and blew it out. "Why are you wearing your tutu as a top?"

She waved her arms up and down to fluff out an extra layer of black tulle. Jagged holes she'd cut into the skirt with mom's kitchen shears bit at her skin, especially under the armpit.

Tis the life of a genius fashion guru, pain and beauty.

"We've been over this, Stefan. This is my mourning tutu. Hence the black. I'm mourning the fact that my almost-friend Willow shall never be my true friend since the clown incident."

"Your mom forgot to run the load of laundry again, didn't she?"

"Are you saying I don't have other clothes?"

"I'm saying you wear weird clothes and then get embarrassed when people think you're being weird for wearing weird clothes."

She drew a pillow up to her chest and munched on it for a moment. "I know . . . me in this tutu, me in clown shoes, it's me, and it's fun. And each time I wear it, I hope I can own it. Like those runway models." She fluffed her hair and then collapsed back onto the bed. "All our teachers say to 'be yourself,' but I really think they mean, 'be normal.'"

Stefan paused and waved at someone off-camera. A large man, Stefan's dad, appeared in Stefan's screen and nodded at Charity. "Hi, Charity. Just letting Stefan know I'm heading out for a tennis doubles tournament." He waved a racket in the air. "I asked his mom if she could take care of dinner. Just wanted to say goodnight in case I'm back late."

"Go get a touchdown!" Charity pumped a fist in the air.

Stefan's dad winced, chuckled, and then left.

Red LED lights strung above the top border of her room chased each other by her closet. One loose end hung like a limp noodle. It reminded her of the dead snake in her backpack.

One crooked door ajar displayed her remaining outfits that hung loosely from hangers. Many had dropped to the green carpet. All that remained: her dinosaur onesie (*we don't speak to him after the detention and wrist-cramp incident*), two pairs of pants with no tutu-top to go with them, and ugh (*shudder*) a normal black t-shirt.

24

"Never mind, I'm not here to talk about your tutu or questionable fashion choices," Stefan said. "I need to tell you something weird."

Charity faced the screen again. She placed the blue pen she'd been doing her math homework with against her lip. Two seconds later, she realized she'd forgotten to put the cap back on.

Yuck. Pen ink.

"Yeah, why's your room all dark?" She squinted at the screen and watched the matching pair of LED lights form a blue halo around his room. Of course, Charity's bedroom was just as dim, but the phone glow could catch the frills on the tutus. With a smile, she fluffed one of the layers again.

"Hoping *she* can't hear me," Stefan whispered.

"Does the darkness help?" She knuckled her lip. The ink smeared.

"My mom."

"Agreed, the woman does have translucent skin in some shades of sunlight, but she doesn't exactly put the boo in boo-hoo, Stefan. Except for the patients she's a counselor for. They boo-hoo a lot."

Charity would know. She met Stefan's mom after Dad left for Phoenix with some lady in red heels and a pink skirt that did not match.

But hey, a lot of boo-hoos helped me to meet Stefan in the waiting room when he waited for his Mom's shift to end.

Her boo-hoo gave her a friend.

"She's, like, the least scary person ever, Stefan."

During Halloween last year, Stefan's mom dressed up as candy corn. Her tufts of blue hair stuck out underneath a yellow square cap. Not exactly a slasher film villain type.

"Why would you be hiding from your mom?" Charity asked

"She acted weird when we drove Io home from carpool. Usually, she stays after for soccer, but her coach suspended her for some reason."

Huh, so the coach went from benching her to kicking her off the team. Did Io somehow bring bad luck to the sidelines? Did Gatorade bottles start exploding out of nowhere?

Charity flicked the page in her math book to the next set of problems. Stefan took five-ever to tell stories, and she might as well get some multi-tasking in.

"You said your Mom did something weird?" Charity prompted when Stefan took an enormous dramatic pause.

"I'm getting to that. Let me build the suspense. When Io went to click her seatbelt, the latch broke off. That metal bit."

Scarlet lights danced on a problem about some guy named Jerry who bought sixty-three apples at a store.

Poor Jerry.

Unless he had some pies in store to bake, he'd have a terrible rotten fruit problem on his hands at any moment.

"Weird. Metal bits. Wow." She frowned at the page. "Anyway, what did you get for number five on the math?"

"Wasn't finished, Chair. Other stranger stuff happened. After Mom had no choice but to make us form a seatbelt with our arms, since there were no other seatbelts in the car, Io reached up to turn up the overhead heater. And the heat went out of the car. Like, it straight-up died."

She quirked a brow and slammed the math book shut.

Thanks a lot, Jerry, for your excessive buying habits. Now I'm never going to solve this math problem.

"But that's not even the weirdest thing."

"Of course it's not." She puffed a warm breath out her nostrils that tickled her nose.

"Mom reached back, sort of in a reflex motion, to figure out the heating situation. Her fingers brushed Io's and the Io kind of shrieked. I mean, I get my mom has cold hands, but seems extreme."

Cold rippled through her fingertips and Charity brushed them against her cookie monster pajama pants. It didn't match the tutu. But one had to make do with limited choices.

Did Mom set the room temperature to 65 again?

Red lights roamed over the white bedroom thermostat. Sure enough, 65. Soon enough she'd have to go for the dinosaur onesie.

"But here's the strange part, Charity." Stefan leaned too close to the camera, and she got a nice view of his nostril. "On our way home, after we dropped off everyone else, Mom acted weird. Granted, I wouldn't want to spend my once-a-week day off work dropping off kids, and losing the heating to her car and a seatbelt buckle, but she was complain, complain, complain the whole time."

Huh, that doesn't sound like Stefan's mom.

Even when Charity, in her boo-hoo session with her,

got purple marker all over the chair cushion by accident, the woman gave a toothy laugh and said she'd put the cushion up in an art exhibit if given the chance.

"And when we got home, I asked her what was for dinner, and she said, 'Don't care. Eat a cookie if you get hungry,' and then she took a nap. So, I guess my dad didn't get the hint. Maybe I can text him to get me Taco Bell." His stomach's rumble faintly fell through her phone's receiver. "Anyway, ten cookies later, I've realized why they say an apple a day keeps the doctors away."

OK, Jerry, you've redeemed yourself.

"I guess your mom had a bad day, Stefan. We all get tired and unkind at times."

"Not you. You may not get the top grades or understand fashion, Chair, but if there's one thing you are, you're kind."

Guilt burbled in her stomach. She had wanted him to get on with the story.

Could've been nicer and let him tell the whole thing. Even if he picked his nose during the pauses.

Stefan cleared his throat. "Anyway, something tells me I might need ten more cookies to make up for the lack of dinner. Some have raisins, so I guess I had some fruit too. Talk soon, Chair."

Shivers ran up her spine when the screen went dark. Her mom had taken a nap too, but un-lucky for Charity, no cookies awaited her for dinner. She'd have to settle for beef jerky and pickle slices again.

Now, to do something about the room heat.

Usually, her mom didn't let her touch the thermostat, but the woman had been taking longer naps than usual. Anything from 6 p.m. to 6 a.m. and one more day without laundry meant Charity couldn't even snuggle up in her sweater with dinosaurs stitched onto the front to bear the cold drafts of the house.

She fluffed out her tutu top, tried to ignore the itches crawling up her shoulders, and stood on her bed. Springs squeaked beneath her weight. She tiptoed over to the wall and slapped her palms against the cool surface to balance herself.

Just need to bring it up to 66.

Teetering, and wishing Mom had not put the bed three feet away from the wall, she jabbed her finger on the triangle arrow that went up on the thermostat. She missed and brushed her fingertips on a part of the LED light string that hung down at a curve.

The moment her fingers grazed the lights, they shut off. Blackout.

Like the heater in Stefan's mom's car.

Chapter 5

Should've Stayed in the Bear Hug Forever....

Three years ago.

Charity sat outside the classroom with her head hunched. A teacher talked in low tones with her mother inside. Probably about the fact that Charity had gone from straight As to straights Fs in the span of a month.

Her dad had left for Arizona one month ago and taken the smarts with him. She was sure of it.

She watched this happen to another classmate when her big brother passed away. The classmate went from As to Cs in the third grade and just now, in fifth grade, gotten a few Bs on the report card.

Charity called this the Big Sad.

Where it felt like someone had plunked her into a vat of Jell-O, and all her movements came out sluggish and behind everyone else.

If her mom had the Big Sad, too, she didn't let on. Even when Charity caught her crying, she would wipe away the tears, grin, and offer Charity the biggest bear hugs.

A door to the classroom slammed, and once again, Mom greeted Charity with a smile that took up her entire face. Brightness filled all of her mother, almost like someone from the Almsgiving Middle School drama club had shone a spotlight on her.

"Hey, kiddo. What say we get some ice cream to celebrate?"

Charity sniffed and wiped her nose on her sleeve. She hadn't realized it had been running these past few minutes. "Celebrate what? I got a bad report card."

Her mom grasped her shoulder and squeezed. "Celebrate that I have a beautiful daughter who is wonderful just the way she is."

Warmth ebbed the numbness in Charity's chest. Some of the Jell-O feeling dissolved and she heaved herself onto her feet. "Think they still have the cotton candy flavor?" Even the grayness from Charity's voice had begun to fade. She and her mom looped arms together, and her Mom skipped down the hallway with her. Tangled braids of red hair flew from both of them.

With her mom, she could do anything.

Even conquer the Big Sad.

Chapter 6

Should've Reined in the Cannibalistic Tendencies. . . .

"Don't eat the other children."

Charity's mom had repeated this mantra to her every single time she'd gone to a co-op extracurricular with other homeschoolers. Perhaps it had something to do with the fact that Charity bit the arm of a girl at co-op soccer because the girl's wrist had some powdered sugar left over from a donut.

But that was first grade, I'm a new person.

This brisk November Saturday was no different.

"Don't eat the other children, Chair."

"No promises." Charity swung open the door to the van and skittered onto the sidewalk in front of the school's entrance. A flag jingled against its pole in front of the squat brick building. She fiddled with a slipping strap on her Bowser backpack, a miraculous feat considering she'd tucked herself into a huge maroon marshmallow coat.

Sure, November in Ohio didn't dip much below forty degrees, most days, but she had to hide the embarrassing outfit underneath.

A plain black t-shirt and jeans.

Sure, it's going to draw no looks. But it's the least me-thing possible. That makes this fashion disaster so much worse.

But hey, at least she'd try to make the world a better place today. Maybe someone in detention needed some extra lead for their mechanical pencil or to borrow her calculator for their math homework. She came prepared for either case.

Exhaust puffed from the van's tailpipe as Mom sped out of the lot. As she turned right onto the main road, Charity spotted the silhouette inside rubbing the bags underneath her eyes.

She spun on her sad, normal, human-sized shoes (Mom had said the clown shoes had gone missing mysteriously . . . *probably for the best*) toward the green-painted doors at the school's entrance. She halted when she almost stumbled into a figure with dark mahogany hair so frizzy lightning could spew out from all the static.

Io! Must've missed spotting her when her mom rolled into the parking lot.

"Io, what are you doing here on a Saturday?"

Her best friend buckled her neck until she shrunk six inches. She pulled out a detention slip.

No, Io got detention? How?

In seventh grade, Io boasted of straight-As, led as secretary on the student council, and was all around the coolest person in Charity's objective and totally not biased opinion.

"It involved a snake incident." Io shook her head. "Basically, someone found out, told on me, and they called me in after lunch yesterday."

Huh. Well, best not dwell on the dire circumstances. They'd endure detention in the only way best friends could, with nonverbal looks of exasperation and laughter.

"Did they lock the doors?" Charity jostled the strap of her backpack with her shoulder and reached for the knob. The door opened with a creak. Warm air spilled onto her rosy cheeks. "Scared? First time in detention? We might get Walterson as a monitor. Fun guy. Likes to pick at his hangnails. I try to take bets on which fingers he'll bite. Bonus points for guessing which digits bleed."

With a cringe of her eyelids, Io stepped away, sat on a bench near the flag pole, and hunched over her detention slip.

"What's wrong?"

"Well," Io sniffed and wiped her nose on her pink hoodie sleeve, "I wanted to text you about this yesterday, but I sort of got distracted by math homework. And Grandma's lectures about snakes. I got a weird note on the back of my slip. I don't know if I should do anything about it though. What will happen if I skip detention?" She hunched into her stomach. Io was a long skinny minny, built like a ruler. Not the best at hugging. But aside from that, Charity's best friend had absolutely no flaws.

"Did Rancor write a fun note in purple pen on your slip?"

"Fun? No. There's something weird about a curse."

"Curse?"

Her heartbeat throbbed like a hummingbird. Rancor must've put the same thing on all the slips.

She rushed behind the bench, ignored the flinch from Io, and peered at the pink paper. Sure enough.

Io,

Miss your friends on the soccer team, since none of them talk to you anymore? Wish that the drinking fountain wouldn't break when you fill up your friend's water bottles? Want to stop the curse?

Meet us at Lake Prespa by the school on Saturday at 9 a.m. sharp.

— The Cassandra Coalition

Io swung her legs back and forth under the bench and then plopped them on the concrete. Dragon's breath trailed from her nostrils in the frisky air, all smoky and mystical.

"Something tells me that they know about all the weird stuff that's been happening," Io said.

"Weird stuff?"

"Yeah, like sometimes when I touch things, they go wrong. Dad's cupcakes, Josie's pet snake, the heater in the car yesterday. . . ."

True, Io had mentioned some of those instances at lunch . . . well, at least, about her father's cupcake disaster. Basically, long story short, Charity learned never to mistake baking powder and baking soda.

"Anyway," Io cleared her throat, voice higher, "I figured

if I went to the lake, maybe they could tell me what's happening. But," her slight overbite clasped onto her bottom lip, "I'm worried what will happen if I skip detention."

Crumpling to her knees, Charity swung around her Bowser backpack tore open the big zipper. She threw the snowballs over her shoulder and dug out the one pink piece of paper.

"I got a similar note. Maybe we go check out the sitch at the lake to mix up this rather dull Saturday morning. Besides, they'll probably only give us detention for skipping detention. Schools can only get so creative with their punishments, you know."

Io brightened. "You think that's the worst that they'll do?"

"Worst? Detention's great! You can catch up on sleep, on homework, on your existential crises. Besides, I bet five bucks that next detention our monitor'll bite the hangnails on his thumb and ring finger. Both hands."

"Just his right hand," Io smirked. "Up it to ten bucks, and you're on."

Chapter 7

Could've Brought a Wetsuit to Detention. . . .

Not going to lie," Charity whispered to Io, "when I think of a secret Coalition, I didn't expect a bunch of middle schoolers in togas and gloves."

One, a boy with dreads and a cleft chin, wore a navy blue sheet with a Buzz Lightyear pattern. Everyone else sported some solid color, mostly white.

Another, a tall girl with a raven braid, raven eyes, and . . . a sadly white instead of Buzz Lightyear toga, folded her arms over her chest. Goosebumps rippled up the girl's skin, visible in the pale morning light, but she tightened her jaw as though in a severe effort not to shiver. Everyone else in the huddle wore long sleeve shirts underneath the assortment of toga-sheet coverings.

"Does nine A.M. *sharp* mean nothing to you?" She pointed a finger at Charity and Io.

Rude.

Her voice came out high-pitched and commanding at the same time, like a basketball whistle. She jabbed an index finger at her wrist which had no watch.

"Dearly sorry." Charity curtsied, then bowed. "But one cannot be rushed when making a dangerous moral decision that involves missing out on some hangnail snacking. We came as fast as we could."

The huddle exchanged some raised eyebrows, and the raven girl cleared her throat again.

"Whatever, we'll keep this meeting brief since *someone's* brother didn't let us use his house again because of his stupid role-playing game. And so now we have to stand out here in the cold for this initiation."

She stared down the kid in the Buzz Lightyear toga.

Mist swirled off the dark lake during the tense silence between the two. The girl then straightened, flicked her braid off her shoulder, and returned to the two non-toga-clad students.

"Welcome to the Cassandra Coalition. Where dreams come true and we get rid of curses. Or at least try to." She said this in a monotone. "Name's Danae. Let's get initiation started so I can get back into my dad's car before my Starbucks peppermint hot chocolate gets cold, mmm?"

Danae gestured to the parking lot a windy path and a brown grassy dune away from the lake by the school. Several cars puffed exhaust smoke. All parents ready to collect their kids from the meeting, Charity bet.

Charity counted the heads of those in the clump. Including her and Io, they made twelve.

Surely they hadn't gotten there *that* late. But when the breeze kicked up at her shins, she understood the want to have parents on standby for a ready escape.

Still, the earth tilted underneath her. Gravity pulled her calves in one direction and the other as she fought the swirling mist that clouded her skull. Curses? Dreams come true? Togas? So many questions, especially that last one.

"Not to stall anything, Danae," Io chewed on a shaky lip out of the corner of Charity's eye, "but we skipped detention for this. I think Charity and I would both like to know why you wrote something on the back of our pink sheets before we do any sort of," she shivered, "initiation."

Charity's eyes bulged. "Also did you do it by magic?" How else would it explain how the note managed to wind up on the next paper slip in Rancor's desk drawer.

"Magic?" Io narrowed her eyelids. "Danae literally grabbed my detention slip in the middle of the hallway, scribbled the note, and then covered her face with her hoodie and disappeared into the bathroom. Mind you, it was the boy's bathroom, so she had to run out and then vanished into the mop closet right next to it."

Rose bled onto Danae's cheeks.

A black bird cawed above the backdrop of a gray sky before Danae spoke again.

"As for your note, Charity, it doesn't take much to get Rancor out of his office. I told him some kid had ripped jeans on nearby, and he bolted out of his chair like a rocket. You know how seriously he takes the dress code. Slipped into his office, wrote on the note, and slipped out. Seeing that you were being sent there any minute. Word gets around fast about panic attacks and clown costumes. Anyway," she hobbled from one black sneaker to the next, "as for your questions, we can't answer any until you do the initiation."

"But you just answered a question we had."

"No, I didn't, Charity. Now, for initiation, we need you to jump in that lake."

Charity's gaze wavered over the lake. Feathery wisps of water vapor floated around the edges of the circular body of water. Skeletonic trees, already relieved of their leaves, decorated the edges.

"Lake?" Charity shivered again. "Can't you have us cuddle a chicken or something less drastic?"

Memories from this past August swirled in her head. About Mom yelling at the canoe-stealing man. About the fact that after Charity tried to help a father and son push their boat into a lake that a sudden hole formed at the bottom of the vessel and drowned it.

The first kind act gone wrong, with many more to come. It didn't use to be like that. Ever since fifth grade, her niceness would have positive consequences. So what changed?

Danae's sharp voice drew her back to the lake.

"Usually we just have people take a dip in the hot tub back at Paris's house. But *someone,*" she eyed the Buzz Lightyear kid again, "has a brother who decided to have a Delphonian

Hoplites campaign today and won't, under any circumstances, let us use the hot tub or house today, so into Lake Prespa you must go."

Charity didn't question her anymore.

Lake dunks and chicken cuddles are basically irrevocable in the eyes of the law.

With a shaky hand, Charity undid the zipper on her jacket and felt a fire burn on her cheeks as she revealed the horror of a plain black t-shirt underneath.

Besides, Io needed someone to jump into the lake with her. She'd make the world a better place today by helping a friend do something bold.

With a huff, she unpeeled the straps of her Bowser back-pack and let it slump onto the grass. She knelt beside the bag and whispered, "If I don't make it, I need you to take care of Mom, OK?"

Io bent her knees as she trudged along and kept her pink hoodie on.

They approached the lake side and a stench similar to the overflowing garbage cans in Charity's garage punched her in the nose. Shafts from fallen tree branches poked out of the dark, wispy surface.

A beautiful spot to get a wedding proposal, or a murder.

Depended on the symbolic significance the murderer or future spouse felt at the moment, she supposed. She didn't really know. Most weddings had gotten ruined for her when her dad invited her to his wedding with his new wife.

No, she wouldn't think about that. That only brought

back the Big Sad. And she'd gotten rid of the Big Sad over a year ago.

She glanced at Io as the two of them leaned over the murky waters.

"Count of three?" Io suggested. They backed to give themselves a running start.

"Three point one four." Charity threw her arms back like a superhero. "Mama wants some pie."

With that, she sprinted and plunged into the waters.

Ice electrified her skin. Never mind that Ohio had only recently dipped into the forties, the lake had some other ideas about Jack Frost and nose nipping right as Christmas songs had started to play on the radio show her mom tuned into during the morning school drives.

She sunk into the darker parts and watched the shifts of light pierce the silvery waters. They disappeared into bubbles as a silhouette sank into the surface, Io.

An "eeee" sound filled her eardrums as a light pressure burned her ears and forehead.

Ugh, gross.

She'd hit the bottom. A slimy sponge encased her shoes. Good thing she hadn't popped those off.

Imagine what the surface would feel like in bare feet.

She waited three point one four seconds, seeing that was the proper 'foot glued to the bottom of a lake' time before she kicked off to advance toward the surface.

Right as she did so, something grabbed her leg.

Chapter 8

Would've Rather Gotten Some Pie, But This is Fine Too. . . .

Charity flailed and kicked and screamed until the pressure from her leg released.

Without giving the what's-it at the bottom of the lake a chance to reconsider, she twisted and bounced her legs up and down until she approached the light shafts near the surface at an alarming speed.

Two gasps and splashes indicated both she and Io broke the surface.

They clasped at the dry, dirty bank. Tufts of frail grass moved their way into her fingertips as she pulled herself out of Lake Prespa. Two navy towels from the Coalition members dropped in front of them, and she bundled herself like a sushi. Still, she couldn't shake the cold from the clothes which stuck to her like an extra layer of skin.

"N-now, about our questions?" Io's teeth chattered. Poor thing didn't have a marshmallow coat to bury herself in. "What is this club, and what is this curse thing you're talking about?"

"And can we, or can we not, borrow that purple pen of yours that you used to write on our slips?" Charity gazed at them through slits, hoping she looked threatening enough.

The Cassandra Coalition had huddled together in a semi-circle around the banks of the lake. They bobbled their legs and grasped at their arms. Wind whistled through the bare branches of the trees.

"Sorry, new recruits, but most of us need to get back to our cars and various beverages." Danae rubbed her hands and blew into them. "Keep an eye out for our lunch table on Monday. We'll explain everything then."

With that, the toga huddle broke, and their sheets billowed in the breeze. They wound up the path toward the parking lot.

Charity and Io pressed together to stifle the cold.

"Was it just me," Charity said, "or did some undead creature also grab your leg and try to drag you to the bottom of the lake?"

Io shivered beside her. "Charity, I know I've been friends with you for three years, but I still don't understand what you mean sometimes."

So had she imagined the sensation in the lake? Best not to think about it. Better to think about how to get out of this freezing weather—and eventually how to 'borrow' Danae's purple pen.

"Wanna catch detention and ask the monitor what hang-nails he already bit off?" Charity waggled her eyebrows.

"Might as well. Someone owes me ten bucks."

Chapter 9

Should've Recruited an Army of Unicorn Zombies. . . .

Charity, I'm gonna need you to step away from that cage."

"But you know I like it so much. He likes it, too."

"He's perfectly content in there."

"Fine."

She released her grip on the white-wire rat cage. Not before she waved her index finger at Stefan's blue rat "Aither" and took in the dusty scent of the contents in the cage.

Ah, rat droppings.

"But I think Aither would prefer to sit in my tangled hair and not on that boring ledge. It's the nice thing to do, you know. Let him out of his cage to explore the vast fire-struck mountainous regions."

With a huff, she plopped onto the shaggy family room carpet and watched the blue-gray rat scale the ramp to the top-most ledge on the cage. Aither squeaked and wiggled his nose in agreement.

"Yeah, well last time you touched him and put him in

your hair, he didn't eat for a week straight. Mom says you can't go near him anymore."

She thought back to Io and her so-called "snake incident." Did this Coalition and their curse have an effect on animals too?

Long bits of soft carpet wove in between her fingers.

Right as she grasped the carpet tendrils, they unplugged from the floor and showered her legs like confetti.

Weird. Weren't they pretty stuck to the floor?

Charity patted the carpet scrapes back onto the ground and hoped Stefan didn't notice.

"Speaking of Mom," Stefan punched the On button for his Xbox, "she's not gotten much better from the heater incident. And it doesn't help that Dad's doubles team keeps doing well. He's out, like, all the time practicing."

Didn't Io mention something about the heater incident?

Her mind was still thawing from the lake and hadn't caught up to speed.

"Complain, complain all the time." He pressed a sequence of buttons on his black controller. "Yesterday she was going on and on about some kid who went to see her at the counseling center right before I was born. About how this girl went missing, and Mom felt like she wanted to quit because the parents blamed her for not helping their daughter enough, and so the daughter ran away."

Charity scooped the other controller into her hands, a white one (not quite toga white). She clicked an X button and the device buzzed in her fingertips.

"Mom was saying, 'What's the point? I'm not helping anyone. Might as well quit.' Keeps taking naps. And if I have to eat one more sleeve of cookies for a meal, I will riot. Thankfully, Dad has brought home some pizzas. But he's confused why Mom hasn't felt up to making food."

That would explain the cookie crumbs that covered the blue family room couch nestled in the corner.

Her nostrils wrinkled when another whiff from the direction of the kitchen, one room over, filled the space with a burnt scent. Almost as bad as the sewage smell left behind on her clothes from the lake.

Long at last, she googled how to work the washing machine and did her own laundry. Did mom's too.

"Hmm, she's never mentioned that patient before, the one who ran away." Charity toggled her left stick in a circle to choose her character. A unicorn zombie.

"Client confidentiality. Basically, she can't tell us who she meets with."

"So, she's a spy?"

Stefan's mom had been known to wear sunglasses on occasion.

"You know, Charity, it's hard to tell when you're being serious and when you're not. Are you joking or no?"

"The secret," Charity raised a finger, "is to never tell anyone if you're being serious or silly. If they don't know, they might think you're smarter than you really are."

Stefan frowned. "Who told you that you aren't smart?"

Charity dug her nails into her palms. She blinked away

visions of the ramen-noodle girl and from her report cards from three years back, and then she cleared her throat. "So anyway, confidentiality."

Slurps from Aither's water bottle attached to his cage echoed off the purple painted walls.

"Legally my Mom can't tell anyone who she meets with. That's what confidentiality means."

"Whatevs, Stefan, I'll keep her secret spy identity a secret." She winked, and her unicorn zombie character from the video game plunked Stefan's fire-breathing lizard on the head with its hoof. "I know that if they know I know, they'll have to take you away to a boarding school where you learn wizardry and the importance of uniforms."

She fiddled with the striped tie she wore, on top of a Tinkerbell Halloween costume. The triangle frills on the skirt had frayed to shapeless ribbons from years of use.

"You're so weird, Chair."

"It distracts from the stupid." She tucked her hair behind her ear.

"You're not stupid. Seriously, has someone been telling you that you are?"

His fire-breathing lizard bobbed its tail back and forth on the screen when the character opened a treasure chest. Happy music accompanied the reptilian sway. Charity let out a breath when the screen distracted Stefan.

Maybe he's forgotten, so I don't have to tell him about what that girl said.

Remnants of the Big Sad overtook her whenever she

thought about ramen-noodle girl.

Stefan clicked an array of buttons. "Anyway, if I hear that girl's name one more time, my mom's former client, I might go and join a boarding school. Something tells me the kids there will appreciate Percy Jackson more than those at our lame public school."

"Good. Because we hear the name Percy Jackson too much in this household."

He didn't answer. Instead, his fire-breathing lizard bonked her unicorn on the horn with a scythe.

"Come on, Stefan. You'd look so nice in a uniform and striped tie. Tell me her name."

Slurp, slurp, slurp.

Wowza, Aither had an unquenchable thirst today.

Stefan jabbed his thumb against the X, A, Y, and X keys before he clicked the pause button and dropped his controller. Carpet muffled the fall.

"Cassandra."

Chapter 10

Should've Worn Togas to School. . . .

The battlefield.

The horror of all horrors.

The forsaken place upon which no man dare attempt to set foot.

The lunchroom.

Armed with a scarlet tray that cradled peaches, nuggies, and a cosmic brownie, Charity strode to the center of the cafeteria. She dodged around circular tables and planted herself underneath a square-shaped light that shone brightly on a green square tile.

A skinny minny figure sidled next to her. Io.

Together they'd brave the pizza-scented Febreze the cafeteria ladies appeared to spray the whole place with, loud din of conversations and giggles . . . The horrible feeling of emptiness, loneliness, and some other 'ness' that always came when someone picked her last for their soccer team in gym class or when she overheard sniggers from classmates behind her desk.

"Any sign of them?"

"Nope." Charity scanned the seats through slit eyelids. "Would help if they wore togas to school, too."

Thanks a lot, dress code.

Past the boy bobbling back and forth in a squeaky chair, her eyes landed on a raven braid.

"Found the treasure, Captain!" She saluted Io.

Arm and arm they beelined to the table. She found two open chairs by the boy who had worn the Buzz Lightyear toga, now clad in a long-sleeve shirt, and she spilled some peach juice on the table when she slammed her tray down.

Relief flooded her, and she licked the spilled tart juice off the heel of her hand.

"Do you always show up late to things or—" Danae crossed her arms and raised an eyebrow. And then proceeded to ruin the effect by slurping a chocolate milk carton through a straw.

"Someone owes us an explanation and a pair of clean clothes." Io crinkled the paper lunch bag and dug out a string cheese. "And someone else owes me ten bucks for our detention monitor's hangnail chewing habits."

Charity nibbled on her brownie. "He didn't go for the thumb. Disqualified."

Danae swirled a plastic spoon in her pudding cup.

51

Everyone watched, mesmerized.

"Io, didn't take you to be the stand-up-to-you type." She popped the spoon into her mouth. "You were the second one to dive into the lake, after all." This part came out all thick. Danae plopped the spoon back into the pudding.

"Yeah, well," Io picked at a scab on her arm. Her shoulders bounced up two inches, "Grandma gave me a lecture as soon as I got back home: about the clothes, detention, and once again, the snake. And if I have to hear one more time about how she walked to school in a blizzard—" She shuddered.

A knowing nod traveled around the circle. Charity counted the heads and realized only seven sat at the table, herself included. Maybe the others had a different lunch period. Or went to the other middle school at the opposite end of town. Almsgiving, although not large in population, took up the space of three small towns in terms of land. This meant quite a few middle schools dotted the town's borders. But they could at least boast that their school was the OG Almsgiving Middle School. The Almsgiving Middle School North and Almsgiving Heights Middle School owned nothing on them.

Danae stirred her pudding once more, two times counterclockwise, once clockwise, and then leaned over. She pulled up a sequin-studded backpack and flourished a sheet of light blue construction paper.

"First things first, you gotta read the rules. Can't explain anything until you sign your names at the bottom." She slid the paper on the table, but it got caught on the peach juice. A

52

wet stain covered one of the signatures at the bottom.

In purple marker read the following:

> Welcome to the Cassandra Coalition.
>
> You're cursed. Yay. Congrats. Whoopie for you.
>
> Now, this is a club that meets during lunchtimes and once a week, usually at someone's house. People do have extracurriculars and go to other schools in the city, though, so not everyone can make every meeting.
>
> All right, now for the rules:
>
> 1. No kindness or niceness allowed – Any activity of charity or benevolence always backfires.
>
> 2. Don't talk about the Cassandra Coalition – Bet you thought this was the first rule, punk. Think again.
>
> 3. Always wear gloves and minimize physical contact with others.

"Wait a moment," Charity jabbed an accusing finger at Danae's naked and quite scandalous hand, "you're not wearing gloves now."

"And what do you mean cursed?" Io set the paper back on the juice puddle. "And why can't we be nice, again?"

Danae pinched her thin nose.

Behind her, a boy in a football jersey guffawed over some joke.

"As for the gloves, dress code. And for your question, Io, every kind action we do backfires. *Especially* when we make physical contact. Happy?"

Electricity jolted in Charity's brain.

It does and doesn't make sense.

After all, when she touched the clothes in the hamper to do laundry for mom, everything turned pink. When she made physical contact with the peanut butter treats, they gave her classmate anaphylactic shock.

Wait, what about the lights the other night?

When she stood on her bed and the LED red vanished from the room.

Then again, she had gotten on her bed to turn up the heat . . . as a kindness to herself.

I guess being kind to yourself counts, too.

Io leaned back and folded her arms over the unicorn cartoon on her t-shirt. "But that doesn't make sense. Just because we all seem to get bad luck doesn't mean we're *cursed.*"

The last word trailed off her lips in a thin whisper. Almost like she didn't quite believe it. Danae tapped the paper with a purple marker, like a wand. Then she rolled the utensil to Io and Io caught it before it trundled off the table.

"Sign the paper and I'll show you."

Charity and Io exchanged indiscernible expressions, and Io beheaded the cap on the marker. She signed the I in her name with a heart and Charity did the same. Except Charity's came out like a deformed Pac-Man.

With a clean swipe, Danae snatched the paper and stuffed it into her sequin backpack. With no ceremony, she shoved her chair back and leaped to her feet.

"You see that sad boy over there?" She motioned to a student in a red t-shirt, alone at a circular table. He sat underneath a banner with the bubble words "Core Values: Friend-ship."

Everyone nodded. Some part of Charity wanted to go over to him and either offer a hug or a dinosaur joke she'd heard from a YouTuber the other day. She had, after all, not made the world a better place today.

Yet.

"The kind thing to do would be to offer him a treat. Comfort him in his loneliness." Danae, with that improper hand, slapped her palm on the wrapper of a six-pack of mini powdered donuts. "Let's see how this experiment plays out, shall we?"

Pressed to the edge of her seat, Charity watched Danae flounce from the table toward the back corner of the cafeteria. When her shadow loomed over the boy, he flinched. Almost in anticipation. She slid the donuts in front of him, gave a brief pat to his bare arm, and sashayed to the Coalition table.

Charity then glued her eyes on the boy with the donuts.

Worms squirmed in her gut. Something in the atmos-pheric pressure of the cafeteria, if the cafeteria had any at-mospheric pressure, shifted. Storms were a-brewing in the most Scottish sense of the word.

He popped three donuts at once into his mouth. Pow-ered sugar decorated his lips and cheeks like a weird shade of lipstick and blush.

Then, the inevitable.

The boy clutched at his throat and gagged. His face harshened to a deep red and the cafeteria lighting glinted his watery eyes. Crisscross apple sauce went his hands against his Adam's apple.

Choking, and for realzies.

A bald man in glasses, their cafeteria monitor, rushed over. He forced the boy to stand and applied a thrust to his stomach from behind. Five sucker punches to the gut later, and a glob of food soared over the tables and landed on a girl's milk carton. Besides the girl's scream, the cafeteria had fallen into a hush.

Everyone at the table had turned back to Danae. Their fearless leader firmed her jaw.

"See? Cursed." She glanced at her hands. "And from the looks of it, it's getting worse."

Tingles ran up and down Charity's fingers.

Yowza, these bad boys could take out anyone. I guess I'll be needing to write more of those funeral speeches, after all.

"So," Io bit a trembling lip, "how do we get rid of it?"

Danae slumped into her seat and ran her fingers up and down the sequins of her backpack in a soothing motion. "Great question."

Chapter 11

Could've Gotten Killed, But Alas, We Get a Boring Weekend Instead. . . .

By next Saturday, Charity had already broken one of the Coalition rules. But Stefan had acquired the professional skills of persuasion, not unlike a sorcerer or a mom with an expired coupon.

How he cracked her went something like this:

CHARITY: Stefan, I have a secret, but I'm not allowed to tell you.

STEFAN:

CHARITY:

STEFAN:

CHARITY:

CHARITY: OK, fine, fine, I'll tell you.

So she did.

In my defense, he'd seen the detention slip and had an inkling about the Coalition.

Stefan cupped his milkshake glass and stared at a group of kids who perused games on the shelves. Ye Olde Pawn Shoppe, their town's beloved spot for tabletop games, milkshakes, and the occasional adult men clad in knight's armor for LARPing purposes, was, as the newspapers described, "A pimple on a pubescent face of a city."

Just kidding, Almsgiving loved anything quirky and full of vibrant color. They actually describe the shop, in very boring terms, as, "A nice place to play games."

The building smelled like wood and several hundred decks of cards.

Stefan stooped to slurp out of his straw, and a dollop of whipped cream caught the tip of his nose. "So if the club doesn't know how to fix the curse, why are they having you meet here again? Don't you have basketball practice?"

"*Coalition* not club," she said this with an air of significance, "and they're working on that part. The whole un-cursing us. For the time being, it's what your mom would like to call a support group."

"And?"

She hunched over her blue-dyed milkshake. Chewed on her lip. "And they kicked me off the basketball team. Too many missed practices, even without the detentions." Charity could never convince her mom to wake up from her long naps and drive her to school on Saturdays for practices. She only drove her for detentions, since the school threatened suspension if Charity missed too many.

Whoops. Probably shouldn't have come late to detention

last Saturday. The monitor really didn't seem to mind, though. He seemed more concerned that Charity and Io arrived dripping wet. But thankfully didn't ask many questions.

And besides no one on the team wanted to give Charity a ride. "It's fine, though. I felt alone at basketball."

Her friend nodded. "Told you. The meanest of sports. They didn't need you." He winked with both eyes.

Rolling her pink gloves into a fist, Charity rested her chin on her knuckles.

Good thing Mom didn't want these bad boys after they got pink-i-fied in the washer. At least I can get one Cassandra Coalition rule right.

The 'no hugging' (physical contact) one would be hard.

Stefan appeared to read her mind when she refrained from engulfing him in a bear hug at the door of Ye Olde Pawn Shoppe.

Of course, she'd halted from doing this prior to the curse. Stefan didn't like hugs. Or touch. Or butterflies.

"Why?" Charity had once asked him. "Butterflies are cool."

"Yeah, and they eat dead bodies. No thanks."

"Doesn't that make them more special?"

Stefan had shrugged."Charity, you would love a centipede because it was different from the other bugs and had a billion legs. It's in your nature. You love unlovable things."

False, she'd wanted to say, *I don't love myself.*

A fah-lap of playing cards on a nearby table brought her back to the Pawn Shoppe.

"Being cursed isn't all that bad. People never asked for

my hugs in the first place. I guess not much has changed, except I wear pink gloves now. Except at school, thanks to the dress code."

"What I don't get," Stefan grabbed the laminated menu on the table and made a fah-lapping noise with it, just like the cards, "is what connects all of you. The cursed ones. I mean, there's twelve of you, some go to different schools. I guess you're all the same age, thirteen. And you live in the same town. But what," he slapped the menu onto the hightop table, "connects all of you? I mean, why did the curse choose *you* of all people?"

She shrugged and scowled at how the paper straw in her milkshake cup had shriveled on her tongue.

Before she could get an answer out, the bell to the door played the Star Wars theme. An older woman, with snow-white hair and large square-rim glasses—Io's grandma—escorted Io and Buzz Lightyear boy inside. Charity waved to Io's grandmother. After Io's grandma parroted the gesture, the woman spun around and her arms wobbled as she tugged at the heavy door.

Everything inside Charity wanted to bolt from her stool and hold open the door for her. But even with the gloves, she would break another of the rules: no kind actions. The curse could somehow find its way through the thin cotton fabric, she bet.

Her heart sank as the elderly woman at last tugged open the portal to and from the shop and disappeared behind the bang of wood.

A tap on the table drew her back to Stefan. He jabbed a thumb over his shoulder at a curtained room. Scarlet drapes separated the normal nerdy customers from the dedicated costumed geeks on the other side.

"Sounds like the Hoplites are ready for me. You still fine with Mom picking us up in a few hours, Chair? The campaigns can go a little long."

Her lips twitched. She gestured at the bookshelves full of board games.

"Even when the Coalition meeting ends, I'll have plenty to do. If not, I can always catch up on writing some eulogies on recycled napkins."

He didn't appear to hear the last sentence as he'd popped off his barstool and raced toward the crimson curtains. They swallowed him up.

Moments later, Io supplanted his tabletop throne. She cradled a green milkshake with red gloves.

The other Coalition member arrived a moment later. He clutched a lightsaber-shaped popsicle.

"Buzz Lightyear, you're here early too?"

"It's Paris."

Paris Lightyear, short in stature, grunted as he saddled the stool. He returned to his popsicle that had already turned his tongue blue.

He stopped, slurped, and stared at Charity. "What are you doing here early? Coalition meeting doesn't start for another thirty minutes. And something tells me Io's grandma didn't need to drop you off early to get to her quilting meeting at church." He threw a pointed look at Io, whose neck had shrunk into her shoulders like a tortoise.

"Friend's mom drove me, and he has a Delphonian Hoplites campaign. He has one here every Saturday. I guess it's the latest craze next to washing your hands and refusing to apologize."

Paris cocked his head and then grimaced at Io. "Is she joking or serious? I can't tell."

Io shrugged. "That's the fun of it. You never know. And we wouldn't have it any other way."

Warmth filled Charity's gut. She and Io shared a glance, and they tele-bubbled an unspoken language to each other. One they'd learned since that fateful Vacation Bible School, years back.

Charity hugged her sides. What a blessing to have such wonderful friends.

Flurries covered the pavement outside a yellow-tinted window.

All three of them appeared to watch the snowflakes, mesmerized. Charity tore her gaze away and nibbled the milkshake residue on her cup. She paid six bucks for this and would get her money's worth.

Well, her mom's money's worth, but Mom only slipped a twenty into Charity's dinosaur-shaped handbag every so often.

"Think Danae'll cancel?" Io licked a green hat-shaped Lucky Charm on the whipped cream of her shake. The bartender had dabbled on loads of dehydrated marshmallows like sprinkles. "The weather looks really bad."

Of course, Ohio chose to snow on a non-school day.

Paris jerked his chin to either indicate no or because some robot overlord now controlled his reflexes. "It's Danae. She'd make us stand outside when there's a tornado a few miles away. Trust me. I know. Because she *literally* made us stand outside when there was a tornado a few miles away."

Io frowned at a green glob of milkshake that had found its way onto her pink hoodie. She brushed away the spatter with her glove.

"No offense, but I don't think Danae would have a hard time with the no kindness rule." Io returned to the Charms. "She's one of the most intimidating people I've ever met."

"Believe it or not, she was actually really nice before she realized she had the curse."

The girls' eyebrows skyrocketed.

A Doctor Who theme blasted out of the speakers when Paris took a dramatic pause. He brightened. Perhaps to soak in the newfound attention he'd gained. Or because the light fixture above his head, which looked like the Eye of Sauron from the Lord of the Rings movies, stopped shuttering.

"Yeah, she used to help ladies cross the streets downtown, bake cookies and give them away for no reason. You name it."

He reached for a deck of cards on the table and split the stack in half. Paris attempted to shuffle them, but in wool mittens this proved to be a trial, and he gave up.

Charity returned to her chin-on-knuckles position. "So

what happened?"

"Eh, the curse does that to you." Paris slurped on his popsicle. The blue dye had begun to bleed onto his gloves. "It's hard being kind when your kindness isn't wanted, or worse, hated."

Chapter 12

Could've Written a Foreboding
Note in Comic Sans. . . .

So as much as I love spending my Saturdays building card castles," Io tried to pick up a stray card that had fallen from the 'moat' on the Coalition Card Castle. The Queen of Hearts wouldn't get unstuck from the long, varnished wooden table at the center of Ye Olde Pawn Shoppe, "I'm missing doing a ton of homework assignments for this. When are we getting to the 'getting rid of the curse' part? I jumped into a smelly lake for this, you know."

Paris placed two triangle cards to finalize the tower.

"Yeah, about that," he sighed when the triangle flattened, "we used to try and uncover the mystery in our first meetings. But that was months ago. And when we didn't get far, we just decided it was a group we could eat lunch with and build card castles."

"After all," he plucked a knight from a broken chess set on the bookshelves and placed the piece in front of the draw-bridge. "Most of us don't have friends outside of this group. If we did, they deserted us when they noticed the bad luck that followed us."

Charity's gaze roamed to the crimson curtain. Behind it, a handful of players, male from the sound of their din, shouted.

How long do I have until I'll lose Stefan, too?

"Buzz-er-Paris?"

"Yes, Charity?"

"Why aren't we wearing togas?"

"It's not initiation day." He paused. "And, Dad threw out the Buzz Lightyear sheets because I ripped them."

A tragedy indeed.

Crimson curtains burst open, followed by Stefan's guttural yell. He raced toward Charity, and she could come to one of three conclusions:

1. Stefan's campaign for the Delphonian Hoplites let out early.

2. Stefan had come to his senses that the Delphonian Hoplites club was a pure waste of his time and talents, and he'd better explore other more practical hobbies like beetle fighting or ferret racing.

3. The ghost from his bedroom, that Charity swore she saw on their video calls, had decided to haunt Ye Olde Pawn Shoppe. At least it smelled like butterscotch here rather than the weird popcorn scent from Stefan's room.

She knew the most obvious answer.

"Give me one minute, Stefan. I can convince the bartender to give us a mirror to catch the ghost."

"What?" He panted, palms clasped on his knees.

The Cassandra Coalition had all but dispersed by now and left behind a wreckage of cards on the table. Charity, Io, Paris Lightyear, and Danae had hung back to collect them and put them back into their cases. With gloves, this added an extra ten minutes.

"I mean, we could let the ghost stay. Maybe she could take your spot in the Hoplites campaign and you could do something else during your Saturdays?" Hope clung to her voice.

He frowned and shook his head. "Just going to ignore the Charity-ism."

> Charity-ism
>
> /chair-itty-ism/
>
> Noun
>
> 1. Something Charity says that baffles all explanation, but asking her for an explanation would make the person who asked it even more baffled. A lot of baffling.
> 2. Something Charity says that you simply nod and laugh and move on with your life, because, no, we don't think even she understood what she said either.

"Anyway, I found something creepy and disturbing behind the red curtain, and I think you should take a look at it with me."

He knows me so well.

"You know I'd love to see it more than anything. But don't they have a campaign still happening in there?"

"Yeah, but they killed my Toxotai. Hemlock poison. Gonna take me too many rolls to re-spawn. Besides," he jerked his chin at the curtain. A group of teens and tweens, some wearing leaf wreaths around their ears, clustered around the bar, "They're taking a break. Best chance to explore paranormal activity, when someone downs a butter beer."

Agreed.

She reached for his arm, paused, then clasped her fingers together.

When they approached the curtain, her heart vaulted into her throat. Here she was, nerd level one, in front of the one layer of thick community theater fabric that separated her and the holy of holies. The game room. Meant for nerd level 20 or higher.

With ceremony and a bow, Stefan swept the curtain back with his arm and she saw . . . a table. A long wooden table with some varnish slapped on the top.

Disappointment caused her shoulders to drop. She expected at least a dark lord in a black cloak nestled in the corner practicing his evil laugh or monologue.

Instead, wooden picture frames decorated the fake stone walls. They contained winner's names from previous tournaments and campaigns held in this room.

Stefan dropped the curtain, and the light vanished from the room. Dim glows from a Poke-ball lamp illuminated the slick lacquer on the table. She followed her friend to the corner nearest to the light source and he tapped his index finger on the edge of the table.

"I'd never noticed this before because I usually sit over there during campaigns." He motioned to the opposite end of the table. "But because my Toxotai shot a minotaur in battle . . . well, you know what happens then."

I do not.

She nodded.

"Anyway, check out what I found when I switched seats with the shield-bearer."

Transfixed on the spot where he left a fingerprint, she glimpsed something tan amidst the dark brown varnish. Whoever carved the writing into the table had used a sharp utensil. In jagged font, the message read:

Beware Semele Park.
— Cassandra

I got a good feeling about this.

She followed Stefan out of the room and squinted at the shift in light. Once her pupils adjusted, she had to restrain herself from tugging his sleeve.

"I have no idea what we just saw."

Whites showed in Stefan's eyes for a moment. He squeaked a wooden chair back and straddled it. "It said Cassandra. Remember? My mom keeps going on and on about someone named Cassandra. Maybe she got abducted at Semele Park or something instead of running away."

Her thumb went to the crook in her cleft chin. A nice resting spot for it, not unlike a hot dog bun to a hot dog. "Hold on." She sat in a chair opposite him. "Although there's nothing quite like spicing up a weekend with an abduction, why would she get kidnapped, ask her kidnappers to release her, and then come back to Ye Olde Pawn Shoppe to write down about the dangers, and then let them re-kidnap her? Besides, in thirteen years, don't you think there would be some other girl in this town named Cassandra?"

Although they did live in a small town, parents did have to get clever with names. Io, Paris, Clementine, Maple . . . her stomach gurgled.

Maybe those last two on the list are what I'm hungry for and not real names.

By now, Io had finished tucking the last card into a deck.

"I know it sounds crazy, Chair, but with my mom talking about that patient, and with you being part of a club with Cassandra in the name, this can't be a coincidence. I mean, look how creepy that font is!"

Tis high in the creep factor.

"Why do you guys call yourselves the *Cassandra* Club anyway?" Stefan pointed out.

"*Coalition,* and it's like Danae said—"

Charity jolted in her seat. She hadn't realized she had an Io perched on her shoulder.

"—we're named after a cursed Grecian princess who would foretell terrible futures for people, and they would never believe them. Basically, we're like bad omens people ignore."

A vein popped out on Stefan's forehead. This happened when the words Ancient Greece crossed someone's lips. "Coalition, Club whatever," the vein disappeared, "even if the Cassandra who went missing has nothing to do with your . . . whatever you call it, if this Cassandra is the same one who went missing, and we figure out what happened to her, that could get my mom out of a funk. I've had to cook for myself you know."

She wouldn't call peanut butter and pickle sandwiches slaving away in the kitchen. But Stefan's mom did have a weird gray tint to her skin when she drove them to Ye Olde Pawn Shoppe that morning.

Io cocked her head. "So how do we fix this curse thing?"

Charity explained about the note found on the table. "Maybe if we head to the park, we can get some clues about Cassandra or the curse. Or at least, maybe we'll find something a geocacher left behind." Ah, the joys of modern treasure hunting. "But it's better than sitting around and playing with cards."

"I like the idea. Where'd we even find clues?" Io picked at a stain left on her pants from the milkshake.

"Maybe the graffiti?" Stefan suggested. "There's tons of it all over the park. Cassandra could've left us a note in spray paint."

Io shrugged and gave up on the efforts of getting a stain off with gloves. "Sounds like a plan. Great work, Charity!"

She clapped Charity's shoulder with a gloved hand, and Charity felt heat bloom in her cheeks again.

Huh, so I could have good ideas from time to time.

Paris slid into the last seat at the table, and Danae waited by the yellow-hued window. Every few moments, she slid her cell phone out of her pocket. Io filled in Paris about the park plan.

Stefan stared at a group of girls playing Candy-land on a table near the door. "Lucky for us, Semele Park is a few blocks down the road. The benefits of downtown being so small."

Indeed the downtown boasted of squat brick building shops, a clock tower shaped like a rocket, and Grecian pillars. A perfect Feng shui disaster. How Charity loved it.

He stood, chair a-squeak, and thrust his hand over the center of their table.

"Now who's with me?"

Io and Charity exchanged a shrug and a smirk and hovered their hands over Stefan's, avoiding physical touch.

To heck with it. We already got cursed, so with all members of the Coalition, we can shake hands, fist bump, punch each other in the face. All three. Whatever the situation calls for.

Paris, stationed nearby, straightened, shoulders pulled back as though someone had tied a scarf around them. He shoved his palm on top of Charity's hand, beamed at them, and said,

"No."

He pulled back his arm, as though singed, and jerked his chin at Danae.

"I can get a ride with her dad. No offense, guys, but we've spent months trying to figure out the curse. Danae named the Coalition after Cassandra when she found a book at the Alexandria Book Shoppe that talked about that Ancient Greek lady. Not some girl who disappeared over a decade ago. You're probably wasting your time."

Charity shrugged and dropped her arm.

"Well, that is what we do best."

Chapter 13

Should've Brought Ectoplasm Spray Paint. . . .

You'd think, being in a small town and all, that they'd clean up one of their only parks."

Io buried her nose into her handmade purple scarf and gestured at the swings set and benches covered in various shades of graffiti. Most of the paint had washed off from the actual playground equipment, leaving behind gray splotches. In fact, the only color appeared to come from the fresh doodles and defacements.

How strange. Nothing else in Almsgiving was gray. This whole park felt very un-Almsgiving.

Charity tried to look cool and stuff her own nostrils into the thing wrapped around her neck. A yarn dragon biting its turquoise tail.

"Well, you know what my mom says about *small* towns," Charity said. "'They can get away with *big* stuff.'"

A car whizzed by them as they stood at the end of the path that led to the park. Water from a near-frozen puddle splashed Charity's right hand. She shivered away memories from the lake and tore off the glove with her teeth.

Best not touch anything for now.

They trudged up the short path into the haze that decorated the playground. Gravity tugged at her legs, as though this place had stuffed her calves with the barbells her mom used to lift for home exercises. Energy had disappeared from her chest and caused her eyelids to droop.

Huh, weird. Didn't she have the same feeling at the lake during initiation?

Moisture from the descended clouds filled her nose, despite the dragon scarf's best efforts. Everything smelled and tasted wet and stale at the same time.

"What do you think we should be looking for?" Io shivered when she passed by a huge, fake rock made of plastic. Little (faintly) green 'stones' nailed to the rock formed a path up to a slide. Charity squinted at the gray color on the slide and guessed at one point it could've been yellow.

Gray caution tape formed over the lip of the slide and she assumed they'd covered the thing in the same tape on top.

No one's going down that slide.

It could've been her imagination, but a dim, blue light glowed inside the slide tube.

Static electricity?

Before she could investigate further, Stefan's voice pulled at her attention.

"Not sure." Stefan sniffed. Puffed out a breath. The vapor disappeared into the haze. "Maybe one of these graffiti markings has Cassandra's handwriting.. Cassandra did leave us a note back at the Pawn Shoppe. Who's to say she didn't also put one here? Let's look for her handwriting."

Charity scanned the various scrawlings in red and blue paint.

Some orange paint under the label of 'Splargmaster' declared his love for 'Maia.'

How romantic.

The orange stood out against the now-gray merry-go-round.

Io squatted by a swooping monkey bar set and sifted the mulch with her fingertips. Charity bustled over and realized that if she'd grown two inches taller, and hadn't known about the monkey bar's existence, she would've smashed her skull right into the metal.

Scarlet paint peeked out from underneath the slate color, like a scar.

"Huh, weird." Io rose and held out a thirteen-sided die. Gray, like the rest of the playground equipment. "Stefan, did you drop your Hoplite die?"

He poked his head out in between the rungs of a spider-web-shaped climber and dug his hand into his pocket. Even from ten feet away, Charity heard the unmistakable jingle of dice. "Nope. Got mine here. Someone must've dropped it."

Charity held out a palm. "Ooh, can I have it? I've been collecting random lost items I've found in public to create an art piece. I'm thinking about either calling it, 'The Lost Are Found' or 'Random Lost Items I've Found in Public.' Can't decide which title has more pizzazz."

With a smirk, Io plopped the die into Charity's hand. It was promptly stuffed into her coat pocket.

"You know," Io flipped over a rubber swing to check the bottom, "it's weird. Grandma and I used to go to this park all the time. We stopped coming a while ago, but I don't remember the paint being so faded. Or all of this graffiti."

Mulch kicked up underneath Charity's rubber ducky boots. They weren't exactly fit for winter, but all the seasonal footwear came in boring black and gray shades. Not unlike this park.

Perhaps the same people who let this playground fade to grayscale had taken charge of the town's shoe supplies. She hoped not. This park reminded her of the Big Sad, where everything would turn gray.

Charity approached the 'rock' and knocked her knuckles against the surface. Hollow. She ambled to the edge and swung her head underneath the side. Then she entered the structure. The hollow fake-rock had formed a fake-cave underneath.

Inside the 'cave', red graffiti covered a plastic tic tac toe board.

She slumped to her knees and let the damp dirt dig into her pants fabric.

Shadows from the 'cave' rendered the writing indiscernible. But a certain dash and a C caught her eye. She squinted and leaned closer to the wall to catch the writing. A loss of balance caused her to lurch forward, and she caught herself with her palm pasted against the wall. Her hand covered the writing.

Her right fingers budged a few inches and she made out the inscription at last:

Find Alexandria.
— Cassandra

Despite the gravity that pulled at her chest, eyelids, and legs, she choked as her heart leaped into her throat.

I did it! I discovered Cassandra.

She smiled and blinked away some wetness in her eyelids.

Maybe Stefan's right. I'm not stupid.

Nostrils wrinkling, she squinted at the note in the darkness again.

Wait a moment, Alexandria?

As in the bookstore a few blocks up main street? Or the almost-friend from Charity's class who liked sparkly hair clips.

Nah, Cassandra disappeared thirteen years ago. She wouldn't know Hair-Clip Alexandria.

"Io, Stefan, I found something juicy. I'm finally smart and can do normal people classes."

Even her voice had lost its color. As though someone had pressed the monotone button. Weird. That hadn't happened for over a year.

She unclasped her palm from the wall, and her fingers retreated back into the coat pocket.

Two silhouettes appeared at the mouth of the cave. Stefan and Io hunched as they entered and the former reduced his eyelids to slits.

"Well, where is it?"

"I know it's dark in here, Stef, but you need to get your eyes checked. It's clearly—" She gestured at the wall, but the red graffiti had disappeared. Instead, a gray slab of plastic had replaced the writing. "Wha-but it was just there. A note from Cassandra."

Well, it *was there* until . . .

. . . until I touched it.

Somehow her ungloved fingertips made the writing disappear.

Great, way to go, Charity.

She squeezed her eyes shut.

Cold pierced her forehead. She buried her nose deeper into her dragon and stared at the wall. Pure hope and adrenaline faded from her heartbeat.

I ruined everything, like always. Stupid, stupid.

A buzz echoed. Stefan dug into his pocket and produced a cell phone.

"Looks like Mom can't pick me up. And Dad hasn't been answering any texts. Any chances your grandma could drive us home, Io?"

Io nodded and slumped to her knees, as though gravity too had a heavy effect on her here. "We can stop by the church. It's only a few blocks away."

Her two friends squatted and waddled out of the cave

like perfect leprechauns. Charity sighed and unrolled her palm from her coat pocket. She stared at the gray thirteen-sided die. Perhaps in a former life, or before some cursed individual touched it, it was red. Just like the writing on the wall of the cave.

Thanks a lot, curse.

Chapter 14

Should've Given the Magic Mirror Acting Lessons. . . .

Three years earlier

"Vacation Bible School?" Charity groaned as she plugged her seatbelt in the front seat of her mom's car. Her dad had been gone for over two months now, but when he posted the pictures of his wedding on social media, the Big Sad had overtaken Charity more today than any other day.

Even though her mom had mentioned getting her into a therapist soon and getting medicine to help her feel more happy, they wouldn't have their first appointment for another month.

And the *last* thing Charity wanted to do was stroll into the mega-church in Almsgiving with a burn-your-eyes-out orange t-shirt they sent to all the attendees.

Almost every Christian family in the town sent their children to the church in June for a week's worth of activities. Charity's mom, despite Charity's protests, insisted she go.

"Sweetheart, it'll be good to see people." Her mom winced and she turned the car into the church parking lot. A large steeple shadowed some of the parking spaces. "Whenever I feel sad, I try to make some new friends. That way, when I make them happy, I feel happy too."

Charity scrunched her nose and crossed her arms. She didn't want friends. She wanted Dad back home.

After her mom pulled into a spot, they entered the large pillared doors and registered Charity at the front desk by some very large windows. A teenage volunteer in pigtail braids beamed at her. Charity scowled back.

"Ten years old?" The volunteer confirmed with Charity's mom.

Mom nodded and squeezed Charity in a hug. "I'm so proud of you. I hope you know that. Please have fun, and I'll have ice cream waiting for you when you get out. Can't wait to hear all about it."

Oh. Well, ice cream did ebb some of the resentment that had clouded in Charity's chest. Still, she hmphed and didn't hug her mom back.

The girl in pigtails led her into a large sanctuary. Blue lights covered a dark stage and decorations from various fairy tales hung from the high-up ceiling.

This year's VBS theme was Happily Ever After with Jesus.

The volunteer halted at a row with a cardboard Cheshire

cat cutout. She motioned for Charity to sit on the bench already filled with other kids that looked to be her age. Ensuring wide berth, she parked three feet away from the nearest kid.

A countdown clock appeared on a large projector screen. When at last the number reached zero, teens, dressed in fairy-tale costumes began a skit on stage. Charity crossed her arms and rolled her eyes.

Oh brother, this would be cringe-worthy.

Then a girl dressed in a Red Riding Hood cloak started to pelt Sleeping Beauty with muffins. Charity stifled a snigger with her nose. OK, maybe the skit *wasn't* that bad.

From what she could tell, beyond the microphones giving piercing feedback and one actor who couldn't enunciate all that well, the Magic Mirror decided to trick all the fairytale creatures into turning on one another.

They ended up hurting each other's feelings, and in the case of Sleeping Beauty, she pricked her finger on a chocolate chip muffin and fell asleep.

At last, Red Riding Hood caught onto the plot of the Mirror. At first, she wanted to plot her revenge, by cracking his glass with a scone. But then a wizard appeared on stage right before she could do the deed.

"Red," he said, "I know he hurt your feelings. But it's not nice to repay a wrong with a wrong. Otherwise, we'd all prick our fingers on muffins, fall asleep, and miss VBS."

Another eye roll from Charity.

After some deliberation, Red decided instead to go to the Mirror and offer him some scones as gifts. The Mirror, who apparently had never been given a baked good in his life, about fell onto the stage.

"Why would you do this after all the mean things I did to you?"

Red grinned and turned to the audience, sitcom style. "Do not repay evil with evil or insult with insult. On the contrary, repay evil with blessing, because to this you were called so that you may inherit a blessing."

Huh, interesting.

Red threw her arms up. "That's what the wizard said! So I'm going to repay evil with kindness. And make this world a better place."

A pang formed in Charity's rib cage. What her dad had done . . . that was mean. He gave her the Big Sad, the stupids, and didn't even seem sorry. But what if she wrote him a letter and told him his wedding pictures looked pretty, and his wife wore nice shoes (even if they didn't match her dress)? What if she made the world a better place?

During snack time, which happened right after the skit, Charity noticed a girl who sat by herself at a picnic table outside. Charity sidled to the other corner and realized, moments later, that the girl's tears had blotted the checkered pattern tablecloth.

"What's wrong?" Charity popped a cheesy goldfish cracker onto her tongue.

The girl stared at her, a glaze coating her dark brown eyes. She opened her mouth, then closed it, as if debating whether or not to share the news. Then she did. "My mom died two weeks ago. Dad thought VBS would help me to take my mind off it but," she sniffed. "Sleeping Beauty looked a lot like her."

Although the Big Sad had not dissolved from Charity's head or chest, another sensation took over. Something her mother liked to call the Mom Override - MO. A surge of confidence and the need to comfort, no matter what the person who got the MO felt before that moment.

Like Red Riding Hood in the skit, she'd cheer up this fairy tale creature.

Charity formed her goldfish crackers into a smile formation and then tried to grin at the girl. "I'm sorry. That sounds really sad. Is there anything I can do to help?"

The girl shook her head. Then her lips twitched. "Thanks for sitting with me. For now, that's more than enough."

She spotted the girl's moniker on a laminated name tag they'd handed to each student at the entrance. Io. Today, she'd make the world a better place for Io, so Io wouldn't have to feel the Big Sad forever.

Tomorrow, like Red Riding Hood and the Mirror, she would write a letter to her dad and tell him that she hoped he was very happy.

After that day, who knew? But she hoped she could keep this up forever.

Chapter 15

Could've Invented the Next Winter Drink - Hot Lemonade. . . .

Charity shrugged off her coat. She placed it on a wooden hook in the foyer.

Io directed Stefan to the men's restroom down the hall and motioned for Charity to follow her into a side door that led to the kitchen. The faint whiff of stale danishes and sink water filled the squat room.

"We can wait in here until Grandma finishes." Io checked her cell phone. "Should be done with her quilting group in five minutes or so." She grunted and pulled herself up onto the island counter in the center of the room.

Charity followed suit and took in the surroundings. At least, what little she *could* take in.

This included two silver coffee makers and a bin full of miniature coffee creamer kits on a counter. She sat on her hands and resisted the urge to down all the hazelnut ones.

Io sighed, rubbed her knees, and then squeezed Charity in a hug.

"Sorry." She released. "It's just—not that my grandma was the hugging type anyway—but as soon as I heard about the physical touch thing . . . I thought how horrible it would be to go a lifetime without—"

Charity wrapped her in a tight hug, boa constrictor style.

"No worries, Io, I got plenty of these to share."

When they drew apart, Io popped off the counter and meandered to a silver fridge on the other side of the room. She yanked open the door and pulled out a glass vase with pink lemonade inside.

"The ladies at the quilting club always have something like this on hand. Never mind that it's November."

She reached into a wooden cabinet and pulled out Styrofoam cups. Rosy liquid splashed into the vessels.

"Here." Io handed her a cup and returned to her spot on the counter.

They sipped and a sour, watered-down concoction cooled her throat.

With a thud, Io set her glass on the counter and leaned back onto her palms. "I believe you, by the way. About seeing the graffiti, I mean. I just wonder how it could've disappeared—and don't say vampires."

Charity clamped her jaw. Then she unhinged it and clasped her hands. "It was my fault Io. I touched it with my bare hands."

"You remember what it said?"

"Find Alexandria. Either Cassandra was really into Ancient Burning libraries or there's someone named Alexandria who has our next clue." She shrugged. "Or that bookstore up the street."

Io thumbed her chin and then her eyes lit up. "Probably the third option, don't you think? After all, Semele Park was a place in this town. It probably means the second clue also is in Almsgiving."

Now to find a time to pay Alexandria a visit.

Io nursed the cup in her hands again. "Grandma will be pretty eager to get us home after quilting, and we don't have much time to go pop into the store now. Guess quilting takes it out of you."

"She's old. Being old takes anything out of you."

"True." She hunched over and choked on something. A sob, Charity realized moments later. "What if we're stuck with this curse forever? I don't know how long I could last without being able to hug someone, hold open a door . . . ."

"Leave the hugging to me. As for the rest, you clearly haven't visited that shop enough. Curses always end in books. They have to. It's what curses do." Charity chewed on her lip in silence for a few seconds. "Speaking of, we'll have to find a time to visit Alexandria. Maybe when your grandma hasn't just created a quilt."

Stefan returned from the bathroom and poured himself a glass of lemonade. They watched the digital clock above the coffeemakers until four minutes had passed. Then Io collected the three cups, dumped them in the garbage can by the fridge, and motioned for them to follow her through a wooden door.

Charity didn't know what to expect out of a quilting club.

Would the club members cut strange patterns and paste them together like a weird scientific lab experiment gone wrong? Would they pit the quilts against each other to determine who was the ultimate quilt victor?

Would they chase each other with scissors?

All of these questions and more she didn't find answered because a lone woman parked at a circular table ran a triangle of fabric through a sewing machine. Charity could recognize the glimmer of white hair from anywhere. In the bright fellowship hall lighting, bald spots poked through the woman's scalp.

Rainbows from stained glass windows painted Charity's rubber duck boots as she approached the woman.

"Grandma," Io spoke this when the sewing machine stopped its shutting noise. She advanced two steps ahead of the group, "where are the others? Did the quilting club let out early?"

The woman grimaced at her and the glint of her glasses nodded at the stained glass windows. Snowflakes cascaded like ashes outside. Charity remembered how they melted on her hair when they entered the church into a gust from the heater.

"Everyone decided to take a snow day." The grandma hmphed. Her voice dripped with sarcasm that even Charity couldn't mistake. "Never mind all the homeless ladies who could use a nice quilt. No, siree. Take a day off."

Can I adopt this feisty unicorn of a grandma, please?

"That's awful," Io agreed as her grandmother placed the triangle on a half-done quilt and scooted back her chair. "It's not even snowing that hard."

Grandma grunted as she rose and reached for her cardigan draped on the chair. She threw it over her shoulders. Paused. "Io, dear, do you know what the opposite of love is?"

Io rubbed her bare fingertips on a navy triangle of fabric. She froze. No doubt, she'd had a hard time adjusting to the 'no touching rule'. Charity thought back to their kitchen hug.

"That's easy, Grandma. The opposite of love is hate."

"No."

Grandma raised a finger and jabbed it toward the ceiling. The white popcorn pattern had a few water stains that formed indiscernible shapes.

"The opposite of love isn't hate. It's apathy." She squinted at Io and then the other two. "Not caring, indifference, whatever you want to call it. It makes you tired, lethargic, unaware of the pain of others. It can take a kind old woman and keep her at home, instead of helping to make a blanket for a family without a home."

Remnants of the Big Sad surged back into Charity. Apathy, the word had a horrible touch of the familiar.

Is that what happened to me when Dad left?

Hadn't the Big Sad clutched her back at the park? How the gray atmosphere had forced her eyelids near-shut and calves to trudge forward.

If she remembered right, the Big Sad acted fast and without mercy. What if the same thing was happening with the curse?

Let's hope Cassandra gets us another clue, and fast.

Chapter 16

Could've Asked the Author to Sign a Stuffed Squid. . . .

Two years ago.

Fliers scattered from the table stationed outside of a book shop. An author in a petticoat and steampunk style hat groaned through her gloves. "Stupid wind."

Charity, stationed next to her mom near the popcorn shop, bolted toward the table and chased down all the papers she could. Some had tumbled onto the street where busy traffic whizzed past. But, for the most part, she collected all the leaves she could. Thank goodness, the sun had beat down on the sidewalk today, instead of the usual rainy precipitation they had in the early summer months.

She raced back to the table and set the papers on the billowing blue tablecloth in a stack. The author placed a lotus-flower paperweight on the pile.

"Thank you, sweetheart." The woman adjusted her hat covered in clocks. "I was a bit annoyed when they told me I was doing the book signing outside. Sure, it's a beautiful day."

A cerulean sky blotted out any chance of clouds. "But the wind about took away all my fliers."

On the sheets of paper Charity had just chased down, the author had information about her other books, a picture of her on a train in the very same outfit, and her website.

"Anyway." The author scratched her name on the inside of a book in purple permanent marker. "It's the least I could do." She handed Charity the book with an illustration of a boy, in goggles, on an airplane.

By now, Charity's mother had reached her side, carrying both of their plastic bags full of cheddar and caramel popcorn.

"How much?" Charity's mom brushed flyaway hairs off her forehead. She was already reaching into her purse for her wallet.

"No charge." The author triangled her arm on her hip. "This your daughter, miss?"

Charity's mom squeezed her in a hug. "The lucky mom, yes."

The author smiled. "You've been raising her right. A little kindness goes a long way."

And it had. Ever since VBS with Io, most of her altruistic acts ended in, at the very least, a thank you.

That was, until last August when everything went downhill.

Chapter 17

Could've Existed in a Book Without Curses, but Noooo. . . .

It was a cozy book shop. Warmth spread from the heaters onto the tight, cloistered shelves. Maybe one-fifth of a lunchroom could fill the entirety of this store. Vanilla permeated the hardbacks that lined the back wall.

Charity scanned the rotunda shelves and found puppets and children's books displayed in a neat carousel fashion. In the corner of the shop, a mom read a book to her boy on her lap. A small table with a plate of cookies sat beside her.

Bells tinkled on the door, and Io slipped inside. She stomped out the snow slush from her boots on the mat before she approached Charity, arms still crossed on her chest.

"How were you able to convince your mom to drive you here?" Io reached for her gloves with her teeth and paused. Remembered. Then she shoved her hands into her pockets. "I thought you said she's tired all the time."

"On Sundays, she usually takes me to Stefan's house." Charity chewed on her lip. They'd gotten chapped. She winced at the door. "He'll understand. Usually likes to play video games on Sundays anyway."

"Most of us don't have friends outside of this group. If we did, they deserted us when they noticed the bad luck that followed us."

She shook away the memory of Paris's words.

Stefan's different. He's stuck with me so far with all of my Charity-isms.

Io had already begun to peruse the shelves. Sadly, no graffiti marked the dark wood or the flowers and lanterns that hung from the ceiling.

"Charity, where do you think we should look first?"

"Do any of these books scream, 'Help! I've been abducted by people who also wash away graffiti?'"

"Well, I found one titled, 'Life of Pi: How to Make Math Fun for Your Kids.' Definitely something scary, but not kidnapping-worthy."

Toothy grins split both of their cheeks.

They spun around and faced a carpeted staircase. There was an upstairs and downstairs to the bookstore. And with the way the workers had stuffed the books into every corner of the store, it could take hours to navigate each title.

"I suppose we could ask one of the workers," Charity suggested. "Do any of them have an undead sort of vibe? Like, 'Hi, I like books and also the blood of my enemies.'"

Io's face contorted like she'd been force-fed a lemon. She shook her head.

"How about him?" Io gestured to a large man who leaned

over the front counter. Whoever built the place squeezed the short countertop so close to the Cookbook bookshelves, even skinny minnies would have to suck in their guts.

A walrus mustache hung on his lip, and his brown hair had faded to a silver tabby.

"Him? I don't know. Doesn't seem threatening enough."

"Oh my goodness, we need to find a book, not an omen. Now come on."

Io dodged around the mother reading to her boy and approached the counter. She reached for a bookmark that was stacked in a neat pile, with a dragon on the cover and flinched. Her arm retreated. Charity wished she'd done the same at the park the other day. At least, long enough to snap a photo of the graffiti. Why did she have to go and touch that dang wall un-gloved?

You're so stupid, Charity.

She took a deep breath and held it.

Then Io tapped her knuckles against the counter. This caused the oxygen to leave Charity's lungs. The man behind it had been sorting through some books on the shelf.

He spun around and his grin disappeared into his mustache.

"How may I help you?"

Charity chewed on her tongue because her first five questions had something to do with if the man was secretly an alien walrus in disguise. Best to let Io take the lead on this one.

"This may be a weird question, Mr. Menander," Io peered at the laminated name tag on his lapel, "but how long have you worked here?"

Menander leaned back and bumped against the book-shelf. He uttered a stout "oof" and shuffled to the left, away from the counter where he had more space.

"Isn't that the question? Linda and I started this book-store twenty years back."

Twenty years. Her heart thunder clapped. *Didn't Cassandra live in this town roughly then?*

Io appeared to read Charity's expression. Granted, Charity did bounce up and down like a slinky to help in case Io didn't catch on. Io fluffed out a patch of frizzy hair. The gloves caused the strands to static-electrify. "I know this is a long-shot, but did you ever have a customer who came in here, oh, thirteen years back named Cassandra?"

His features darkened, almost to a shade of gray.

Called it. He's a walrus alien.

"Can't say that I have." He motioned to the main area. At least ten bodies had squeezed in between two close walls of bookshelves. "As you can see, we have many customers come here during any given day. Can't learn everyone's name, even if it is a small town."

Io's ankles budged backward two inches.

"No worries. That's all." She slipped her hand into the crook of Charity's arm and yanked her toward a corner of the store where a cartoon owl poster board with a speech bubble above his head told the customers "Don't forget to purchase a bookmark on your way out".

Io dropped her voice to a whisper. "He's clearly not

telling us something. That means there has to be a clue somewhere. Any ideas as to where we can start?"

She squeezed her eyelids shut.

*Come on, Charity, you already let them down at the park. I
know you're not the brightest, but think . . . got it!*

Eyelids flew open.

"Danae had gotten a book from here where she learned
about Cassandra. The Greek Cassandra, not the vandal Cassandra. Although can you imagine how cool it would be to
marry the two concepts? A toga-wearing, spray-painting—"

"Charity."

"Yes?"

"Focus."

"Right, sorry. Anyway, she got that book at this store.
Maybe we should start there. I think it's a History book. At
least, that seems to be what Paris indicated."

Io nodded and gestured at the staircase. "Bottom level.
Nice work, Charity!"

Charity's confidence buoyed like a balloon in her chest.

They raced toward the stairs and had to duck because
the slanted ceiling by the staircase hung so low.

Carpet muffled their steps, and the smoky scent from a
wall heater stung her nostrils. They dodged around the space
heater and a stack of prodigal books and Io signaled to a book-
shelf at the far corner of the long room. A laminated yellow
label with the words "History Books" gleamed in the glimmer
of wan light.

No other customers occupied the striped couches. The

fabric was ripped in the center of one of the cushions.

The two girls approached the History bookshelves and scanned the spines for anything Greek or something with a catchy title like "How to End a Curse and Work a Smokey Eye Look All in One Day".

Charity's eyes jolted to a stop when they landed on an all gray cover. At least, gray, with splotches of red. Like the graffiti back at the park.

Gloved and ready, she nudged the book out of the middle shelf and yelped when she read the title: "Oracles and Omens: A Guide to Ancient Greek Mysticism and More".

She flashed the cover at Io. "I think we found her."

Io's eye(os) bulged, and she grabbed the book from her. Pages flew through her gloved fingers. "Argh, it's so hard to turn pages with these." She pulled one glove off. Risky, risky. And plucked through the pages. Stopped when she reached one in the middle.

Then she flipped the book over, so the contents on the page faced Charity.

Someone had used white-out to cover the paper. And wrote, in red letters:

Drown.

— Cassandra

Is that a suggestion or—? Maybe Cassandra also likes to say things that sound like she's joking and being serious at the same time.

"This doesn't make any sense." Io nudged a cell phone out of her jeans pockets and snapped a picture of the page. Good thinking.

I blew all my money on the shake at the Pawn Shoppe. No way we could afford this hardcover monstrosity.

"Is she saying she drowned?" Charity asked. "Saying we should drown? Advising us not to overdo it with the hydration?"

"One word isn't much to go off of." Io sighed, re-gloved her hand, and slumped her shoulders. "I think we might've hit a dead end."

Chapter 18

Should've Added Juice Boxes to the List of Deadliest Weapons. . . .

Io: Hey, I think I might have cracked the code from the bookstore yesterday. Meet me at Lake Prespa after school.

Charity's heart vaulted into her throat as she placed her phone in what her Earth Science teacher called 'the cell phone spa.' The clear PVC fabric pouches, attached to the classroom door, held their phones for the duration of class.

With a sigh, Charity slid her phone into her designated phone holder, number thirteen, and trudged to her seat. She could wait one more period. She could—

Outside the rectangular classroom window, she watched a seventh-grader with a huge backpack slip and collapse onto the ground.

Ouch!

The bell rang as she shot to her

feet, armed her back with her Bowser book bag, and raced for the door. Right before the teacher moved to close it.

She skittered out into the hallway and assessed the situation.

Looks bad. Spilled juice box. Cleanup on aisle thirteen.

The victim: a boy with a pineapple-shaped haircut and a gap between his teeth. He grimaced and showed off that little divide in the space-time continuum.

Poor kid.

She leaned over him and extended an arm.

Then she froze and double-checked her fingers.

Yep, still gloved, in the clear.

A miracle, with the school's strict dress code rules. Good thing she hid her hands under her desk most of the time.

"Here, let me help you."

The boy clasped her wrist and arched his back, but a sudden pop caused him to howl. His arm fell slack against the wet tile and he nursed his shoulder with his other hand.

"You did that on purpose!"

"Did what?" Heat filled her cheeks. In her peripherals, she felt the burn of a thousand eyes from the classroom she'd just left. Images from the clown suit day flooded her vision.

The boy's yelp pulled her back into the hallway. Tears squeezed out of the corners of his eyes. "I think you popped my shoulder out of socket."

"But I—but I—wore gloves."

A clean rip sounded from the door of a classroom. Sure enough, the teacher had pulled out a pink pad and scribbled furiously with a blue pen. That meant another trip to the vice principal's office.

I'm going to be late for my meeting with Io, aren't I?

Oh.

Chapter 19

Could've Drowned. . . .

Charity panted and clasped her palms on her knees when she reached the lake. Sure enough, Rancor decided it was a good time to recite what sounded like a bad monologue he'd written for a play called, "Principals and Principles: Why We Must Not Pull Our Classmates' Shoulders Out of Their Sockets."

Calves and chest filled with lead, she sank onto the grass near the banks of the lake and watched the mist hover over the dark surface.

What had she done wrong? She made sure to wear gloves. She'd followed all protocol except—

The kindness rule.

The reason why she could no longer hold open doors or advise her Uncle Ricky against timeshares. Because kind acts backfired with the curse.

She drew her knees up to her chin and puffed out a breath. Snowflakes drifted onto her eyelashes. White clumps bounced once, twice. Twisting her neck in both directions, she wondered where Io had gone.

Unzipping the small pocket on her Bowser backpack, she pulled out her phone and checked the time. Rancor had only held her five minutes over. She clicked the center button, but no texts from Io illuminated the screen.

She de-gloved and rattled off a series of messages to Io.

Charity: Did you get eaten by a zombie?

Charity: If so, how rude.

Charity: You didn't even let me get eaten first.

Minutes drifted past. She occupied her time by watching the different billows of mist cover one another. She imagined each individual wisp decided to dogpile each other, similar to football players. Did vapors have sports programs?

Long at last her cell phone buzzed its usual theme from the movie Psycho. She rolled onto her side, and the light died in her chest. Io had not texted back. Instead, she received messages from Stefan:

Stefan: Hey, Io's grandma is here to pick me up. Guess whose mom is in bed again today . . . .

Stefan: She mentioned that Io had said she had to do something with you after school. Any chance that you both will be done soon?

Her nostrils wrinkled, a boogie or two solid inside from the cold. All of her face had scrunched up.

Charity: What are you talking about? I haven't seen her.

His texts came seconds later.

Stefan: She's not answering her phone.

Stefan: Any chance you know where else she could be?

Mist skirted off the lake and wrapped around Charity's ankles. She surveyed the dark waters and a certain memory of seaweed clasping her legs tugged at her rubber duck boots. Rocks filled her gut, and she tried to blink away visions of the boy in the hall and the clown suit she wore what felt like ages ago. Then, her memory focused on one word.

Drown.

Stefan: ???

She drew in a deep breath, blinked away tears, and tugged her Bowser backpack onto her shoulders. Memories with Io crashed on her like an enormous sea wave. Of the first time they went zip lining together for their classmate's summer birthday party at LifeLine Ziplines and More.

When Io called Charity in tears in the middle of the night because a boy she crushed on liked centipedes, and a boy she liked could *not* like centipedes. It just wasn't natural.

Of their first school choir concert together where Charity's voice box shrieked on a high note, and they laughed about it after over ice cream at The Scoop.

Of their first makeover, sleepovers, and any other -overs.

Then, for the first time in a long time, she let the Big Sad take over.

Wait a moment, the Big Sad. She'd felt it when Io's grandmother talked about apathy. The Big Sad, the curse, Io, the notes from Cassandra . . . all of it added up once the wave smacked Charity down into the grass by the lake.

She texted Stefan.

Charity: I think she might have found Cassandra.

Chapter 20

Would've Colored With Broken Crayons, Too. . . .

Three Years Ago

In the waiting room at the counseling center, Charity filled the petals of coloring book flowers with black and red crayon. A nearby essential oils diffuser puffed lavender smoke.

Two seats down, a boy shielded his face with a Percy Jackson book. He clapped the pages shut and furrowed his eyebrows when his gaze landed on Charity's drawings.

"Your flowers are weird."

She reached in her hair to fluff a braid, but her fingers got caught instead. "Why, thank you."

"You're weird."

"Why thank you, kind sir."

"Name's Stefan, not 'sir.'" He cocked his head and had to lurch forward to catch his book which slid off his lap. "You know, my mom says that patients here have different coping mechanisms when they go through something sad. But I can't tell if you're joking or serious."

Charity bit her lip, and a black crayon snapped in half in her sweaty fingertips. She'd gripped the utensil too hard.

She put the broken crayon back in the box, leaned over a seat, and whispered. "The secret is to never let people know. Maybe they'll think you're smarter than you are."

Stefan frowned. "Who told you that?"

Her words caught in her throat. She considered swallowing them for a moment, like a lodged cotton ball. "My dad."

They sat in silence for a moment. The woman seated upfront reached a ringing phone.

Charity dug into the crayon box for a dark gray.

"Wait a second," Stefan said when she'd procured one, "why aren't you coloring the flowers with the black crayon? They were starting to grow on me."

She shrugged. "It's broken."

He lifted an eyebrow and split open his book again. "Last time I checked, it still does its job, broken or not."

Warmth filled her tummy. She reached into the box and pulled out the tip of the broken black crayon.

"Yeah," she said, "I guess it does."

Chapter 21

Would've Made All of the Undead Feel Included and Loved. . . .

Clouds trailed Stefan's breath. He hunched over his knees and panted before finishing his jog to her by the banks of the lake. "What do you mean she found Cassandra?"

He waggled his chin in every direction, as though trying to force Cassandra to reveal herself in the mist. Stefan scratched at a pimple that nested in the cracks between his two chins. "Where's Io?"

Itchy water filled Charity's eyes. She flopped her arm to gesture at the dark surface of Lake Prespa. Stefan cocked his head until his ear almost reached his shoulder.

"They went for a swim?" He shivered.

"Drowned."

"I'm sorry, what?!"

"That was Cassandra's next clue that we found in the bookshop. 'Drown.' What if Io discovered something in the lake and she hasn't resurfaced?"

She rubbed the streams of water on her cheeks against

her coat sleeve. Mud squelched her rubber ducky boots, and she noticed she sported some brown patches on her jeans.

"So let me get this all straight." Stefan's voice cracked like pubescent thunder. "You think Io jumped into that freezing lake, let herself drown, just so she could join an undead army and locate Cassandra? What is it with you and zombies, by the way?"

"It's not always zombies," she muttered, "sometimes it's ghosts, mummies, and skeletons. Representation matters."

"No matter what race of undead, we need to face the facts. People go boating and fishing in this lake during the summer. If I'm remembering correctly, you went on your birthday this summer and didn't get recruited to rule a bunch of zombie mermaids. If some weird paranormal activity happened, we'd know that by now."

Doubt vaulted into her throat.

Of course, you'd dive to a ridiculous conclusion, Charity.

She sniffed.

You can't be normal like other people and think of real solutions.

Charity held in a breath until her lungs burned. Stefan reached forward to clap a hand on her shoulder. She bristled, and he yanked his hand back.

"Let's say your ridiculous scenario was true, what were you going to do?" Stefan asked. "Jump into the lake and rescue her? Wouldn't the zombie-whatnots get you too? What you need are solid facts and a plan."

He shoved his fingers into his pockets.

"Io's Grandma is searching the school now for her granddaughter. Any clues where else she could've gone?"

She scanned the lake again. Anemic ice had formed around the corners. Overhead, wiry trees dangled their branches over the dark surface.

It doesn't matter. I'm probably wrong. I always am.

She tore loose skin off her bottom lip.

Stefan hocked a loogie behind her. "Never mind. I'm sure she'll turn up."

Chapter 22

Should've Brought Applesauce to a Food Fight, but Tapioca Pearls Will Do....

I o did not, in fact, turn up.

One day away from Thanksgiving Break and the school had already issued an email to the parents about a missing student. The same message also asked if they would consider donating to the school's Chess Club field trip to St. Louis, the chess capital of the world, but Charity assumed the principal did this because they didn't want to fill up inboxes with two separate emails.

Spoon in her tapioca pudding cup, she stirred and surveyed the vacant expressions at their Cassandra Coalition lunch table. The team had taken a hit. No doubt, something to do with the curse caused Io to disappear, and if Charity hadn't helped the boy who slipped in the hallway, she might've found out just what had taken their friend.

Stupid kind urges

A fluorescent light above Danae buzzed on and off like a firefly.

Danae exhaled, popped a hot Cheeto into her mouth, and smacked the red powder on her lips.

"Charity," she winced, "I wasn't completely honest with you. And I told Paris to lie to you for me."

Her ribcage warmed.

In went another spicy Cheeto. "I thought that if we told you we couldn't dig anything up about Cassandra, that you'd drop the search." Crunchy crunch crunch. "But clearly that didn't help." She gestured at an empty chair stationed near a splotched tile. They'd put that chair at their table in honor of Io.

Danae dabbed a napkin on the corners of her lips.

"Anyway, most of what we did find on Cassandra wasn't helpful. People seem to want to hush up whatever happened to her. We know that she was thirteen when she went missing, lived in this town thirteen years ago, and lived on Thirteenth Street. And we have a feeling she may have been the first person to get the Cassandra Curse, making our total membership: thirteen."

Sounds like a pattern. But what do I know?

Danae straddled the back of her chair and aimed her Cheetos bag into the trash. Swish. Charity bet she would've done well on the basketball team and probably wouldn't have apologized for fouling. Danae halted, mid-turn when she spotted a banana peel on an empty table. She shot to her feet, plucked the biodegradable litter, and aimed for the garbage can again.

This time, the banana's carcass soared right over the mouth of the bin and smacked a boy with a buzz cut on the back of his neck.

He loomed over the back of his chair, cupped his hands to his mouth, and shouted, "Food fight!"

Bravely, Charity ducked under the table and hid.

It seemed Danae had the same battle strategy because they landed between the skinny table's legs at the same time.

Chunks of iceberg lettuce fell in between the gap of the table's legs like hail against an umbrella. Charity drew her knees to her chin and eyed the bottom of the table for any gum wads that could get caught in her tangled braids.

"I don't care what that school-wide email said," Danae said. A chocolate milk carton slid underneath their table like a grenade. Danae grabbed the drink and calmly chucked it at the fuchsia leggings of someone nearby. Milk splattered, followed by a shriek.

Charity nodded. "Agreed, the chess club hasn't won a single tournament. Wouldn't it be better to award a trip to St. Louis to a club that's had a higher success rate?"

Danae flicked a wad of spaghetti that got caught to her fuzzy pants. "I meant the part about how they think she ran away."

Oh, right.

Memories from yesterday flooded her amidst the orange juice waterfall that cascaded from their table's edge.

How Io's grandmother paced the front office tile, on the phone with the police to file a Missing Person's Report. About how she chucked the cell phone, with surprising grandmother velocity when they didn't take a tone with her that she liked. And how would Io's dad react all the way in China? Did he know by now? He must.

Charity rubbed the bottom of her eyelids which had grown heavy and itchy from tears of the past twenty-four hours.

Din from the echoing shouts filled her ears with a ring. Two polished shoes stopped in front of their table, heels to them. The cafeteria officer. No doubt, he was investigating the coleslaw confetti show they witnessed from under the table.

"Anyway, I agree with you, Charity. This probably has something to do with the curse, why Io's missing."

She lifted her shoulders.

Maybe I'm not dumb.

"Yeah?"

"Yeah. And I think the best bet to find Io is to discover what happened to Cassandra all those years ago."

"So you'll help me piece it all together?" Charity extended a hand. In between her fingertips and Danae's palm planted on the ground, a chip bag rocketed past. She made a mental note to pilfer snacks to take home when the battle ended.

Danae took her hand, gave a firm shake.

"No."

Charity's shoulders slumped.

"Sorry, but only on a technicality. We'd be helping Io.

And helping means kindness. And kindness means—"

Something slimy smacked Charity in the back of the neck. She unsuctioned the pudding cup and flinched as the mixture oozed down her spine. The echoing shouts withered and hands and arms faded in and out of view as classmates stooped to pick up the stray bits of food and dunk them in the trash.

"—it'll backfire." Danae gripped two legs from the table and yanked herself out and into a standing position.

Doesn't it always?

Chapter 23

Should've Asked the Government to Make Snacks a Currency. . . .

On the downside, the pudding cup debacle ruined the back of her second favorite t-shirt that featured a pirate penguin.

On the upside, she had a new stash of snacks for Thanksgiving Break. Sorry, Grandma Penny, but if given the choice between her cranberry sauce and eating socks . . . .

Then again, her aunt's creamed corn concoction took the cake for worst Thanksgiving dish ever.

On her knees, next to her bottom-half locker, she dumped the treats into her Bowser backpack. Then she scanned her binders. Teachers, freaked out upon the possibility of the lack of learning that would occur between Wednesday and Sunday of Thanksgiving break, made sure to send them plenty of assignments to make up for the paucity.

Two sneakers squeaked next to her and she peered up at Paris Lightyear.

With a hmph, she returned to her big olive science binder. "You."

"Me."

"You lied to me and didn't even tell me." How would she fit all the binders and snacks in the same pouch in her backpack? Ah well. If worst came to worst, she'd forgo the homework for break.

A weird old cheese scent drifted from her locker. Strange. Might have had to do with the bacterial cultures she'd kept in plastic bags at the beginning of the year. She slammed the door shut and grunted as she rose.

When she hoisted her backpack on her shoulders she felt the wet pudding stain from the shirt. She'd tried so hard to wash the fabric in the bathroom sink. And with her mom's track record for doing laundry, goodbye, Mr. Pirate Penguin T-Shirt . . . .

"Look, Charity, I know we're not on the best of terms."

"We're not on *any* terms. I don't know anything about you. Second favorite movie, what animal you'd ride into battle, what kitchen utensils you'd use to replace your hands, no-thing, Pa-ris."

They ambled toward the end of the hallway. Green lockers lined one side of the wall, on the other, watercolor projects from the Advanced Art class.

Paris's shoes squeaked again. "Anyway, I know that Danae isn't going to help you. But I think she's wrong. The curse doesn't really seem to affect us if we're kind to other Coalition members." He looped his thumbs into his book bag straps. "I think she's being paranoid."

Fluorescent lights bounced off Charity's silver glimmery shoes. She'd decided to give the duck boots a rest today after she discovered a hole poked into the toe.

Paris sighed and swerved around a girl hunched near her locker. "What I'm trying to say is, I want to help. Everyone in the Coalition does, really. It's in our nature to wanna help. We're just too scared to."

"But not you?"

"I'm scared, sure, but we'd love to throw fruit into a trash bin without starting a food fight."

He picked a strand of lettuce out of his hair and flicked it.

They curved to the right toward the glass doors. Paris pulled the handle open but didn't hold the door for her. Too risky. Even if they both had the curse.

"And I think I may know someone who can help. I didn't want to consult him before because no one else seemed on board with investigating. But with one of our own taken—"

With a sniff, he buried his nose into a plaid scarf that wrapped around his neck. They reached the end of the path that led to the main entrance and veered to the left. A number of busses had lined the path with cars stationed behind them. The usual pickup spot at the school.

"—you and I are going to crack this." He rubbed his palms together. They made a dry noise.

When had he last used lotion?

"Although he might be tricky to convince. Especially with only one day at the library open before they close for Thanksgiving. Since the library's our best bet in finding info on Cassandra."

He paused next to a maroon car with a white sword sticker on the window.

"But he's the best researcher I know. If anyone can unearth something about Cassandra, it's him."

"Who's him?"

The car window rolled down, burying the sword's hilt into the passenger door. Inside, a pair of thirteen-sided die plushies dangled from the mirror. A large boy, high school aged from the looks of it, clawed at some dark fuzzy beard that had sprouted on his chin. He wore a fleece-lined jean jacket with a Dalek sported on a white t-shirt. Level of nerd, at least a nine, she guessed.

"My brother, Hector."

Hector saluted her with two fingers and clicked a button on his dashboard. Bass throbbed the car.

Paris poked his head and arms into the passenger window and shut off the music.

"Listen, bro, got a research job I need you to do. Library's closed Thursday, and with exams coming up after break, we won't have much time for detective-ing. Any chances you could get us something?"

If Hector had sunglasses, he would have pulled them down an inch on his nose to give Paris an I'm-so-cool-and-you-are-so-not look. Instead, he yanked the monocle off his left eye and attempted the same expression.

Nerd level bumped up to a thirteen.

"Don't do rush jobs, unless you can pay."

"I'm your brother!"

"Exactly, so I know what Mom gives you for allowance. And that isn't gonna cut it."

Either uncomfortable or fearing Hector would close the window on him, Paris pushed himself back onto the sidewalk.

Charity took this opportunity to unzip the large pouch of her Bowser book bag and dump the snack contents stolen from the cafeteria into the front seat. Clear wrappers coating various American delicacies slid from the tan leather seats onto the floor.

"There's more where that came from." She winked with both eyelids at the same time.

Hector perched an eyebrow on his forehead and pinched a bag of chips. He grinned and turned to Paris.

"Listen, bro, be glad you brought this smart madame with you. She knows how to negotiate."

Her belly warmed at the words *smart* and *madame*. She felt so erudite and French.

"All right, now tell me, what do you need me to dig up for ya."

Chapter 24

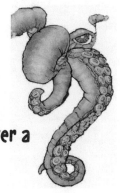

Would've Perferred Death Over a Family Gathering. . . .

Pre-Thanksgiving (Charity's House)

1:36 P.M.

"Charity," her mother pulled a palm down her face, "why on earth are you going to wear that thing to your aunt's house?"

With a grin, Charity wiggled the backside of the costume. A fluffy purple tail brushed against her leg. She reached up and 'pricked' her finger on the iridescent fabric horn.

"Figured that if I go in a weird enough outfit, you'd decide to have Thanksgiving here instead. Out of pure embarrassment of your offspring, and also because a delivery pizza tops that cranberry sauce and creamed corn any day."

Mom's lips twitched and she pinched one of the triangle 'ears' perched atop the hood of the onesie. "Sweetheart, I'm not a huge fan of family gatherings either, but we have to go."

"Why? Everyone there is so . . . mean."

Uncle Nestor often yammered about how his kids disappointed him. Aunt Calypso yammered about how Uncle Nestor disappointed her by always being disappointed with his kids. And as for the cousins, well, their ping pong game said everything.

This made her think about Danae . . . who also wasn't known for her 'nice streak.' Which made her think of . . . wool got lodged in Charity's throat.

Io, I wish I knew what happened to you.

Her mom leaned forward and cupped Charity's chin, rubbing a thumb on her cheek. Charity flinched at the physical contact, but her mother didn't release. "I know, sweetheart. But we go because it *is* kind. Besides, your kindness always appears to perk people up."

"Yeah, well, Grandma can be a tough bundt cake to please." 'Tough *cookie*' was too generous. She went for something that had more of a burnt taste and a hole in the middle.

"I wasn't talking about your Grandma."

Thanksgiving
2:00 P.M.

When they arrived in the basement, two of her cousins whacked hard at a ping-pong ball. Rubber dangled off the paddles from overuse.

One of the cousins, a ruler-shaped teen with a prominent collar bone, smashed the ball at the corner of the table. He missed, and the orange ball rolled under a beanbag chair, nestled in the corner between two scarlet-painted walls. A looming figure in a flowery dress waddled over to the bean bag, stooped, and retrieved the ball.

She then uncurled her spine, at least as much as she could for an older person, and shooed the two cousins away by the flick of her hands. "Remove the net, we're using this table for all the dishes."

Grandma stiffened and waddled to the right to catch a glimpse of Charity.

"Dear girl, why on earth are you wearing that onesie? You'll get gravy all over it. And are those gloves? Take those off before you get cranberry sauce all over the fabric. I know how much your mother hates to do laundry."

Charity's arms shrunk into the oversized white sleeves of the unicorn onesie. She pulled her gloves up to her teeth and tore them off then stuffed them into the pockets of her outfit.

The gloves made her think of Io. Did her friend wear gloves when she stepped into the lake and disappeared from her life forever?

"Now." Grandma cleared her throat with a hack and spread open her arms, bird style. "Come on, darling, give Gram-gram a hug."

Oooh, hug, yes. I like hugs.

Charity mimicked the arm gesture and raced forward, halted, and dropped her arms.

Wait, no hugs.

Physical contact spread the curse. Or at least, she didn't prefer to see her relatives choke on donuts or start food fights.

She glanced at the horrible, gloomy creamed corn dish

her aunt had made.

It could get ugly if someone threw that.

A weird swirl of smells invaded her nose from the kitchen sidled next to the staircase. The huggy aroma of mashed potatoes would've warmed her insides if not for the tart stink from the cranberry sauce. A glass bowl full of crimson liquid-like slush sat next to a circular plate of crackers and cheese.

Her stomach burned. How she wished she hadn't given Paris's brother all of those cafeteria snacks. Should've kept some back for leverage, and/or, alleviation from Grandma's over-exuberance with currants and orange peels.

Grandma's skin faded to a Mom gray. She dropped her arms. "What? No hug? Don't tell me you've gotten all shy."

Pink cheeks showed against the off-white fabric of the onesie.

"How do you expect to get any boys your age to like you if you don't even like giving hugs? Don't you have a crush on someone?"

"No."

"Not even that Stefan boy you like to hang around?"

Blargh.

Mom cleared her throat. Charity had almost forgotten her mom was standing right by a wooden column. "Need any help with anything, Mom?"

"Matter of fact," Grandma said, "I do. Why don't you ladies help me to start bringing covered dishes over to the table?"

All of Charity slumped. Even though her fingertips itched to grab all the porcelain dishes with spoons jutting out of them, she could only imagine how those scenarios would end.

Splat.

Thanksgiving

2:05 P.M.

"It's never too late to start thinking about getting married."

"Mom, she's thirteen."

"Don't listen to her, Chair-Bear. Gram-gram is always right. And you don't want to end up like your cousin Verity, do you? Twenty-six and without a husband. Talk about a spinster."

"Mom, Verity owns her own salon downtown. She makes six figures a year, volunteers at a local soup kitchen, and coaches a rec volleyball team during her downtime. What more do you want?"

"All those accomplishments are well and good. But if she had a husband—"

Mom scoffed. "You just want Charity to wipe down these dishes for you, don't you?"

"Well, it would certainly make her more appealing to young men if she made herself more useful. Besides, I have to carry all these covered dishes down to the basement by myself. What happened to the granddaughter who would trip over her own feet to clean up for us during family holidays?

Don't tell me she's become a teenager."

With a huff, Mom seized Charity's hand and pulled her toward the ping-pong table. She hadn't seen her mother show this much initiative in a while.

For the first time, in a long, long time, she cared.

Thanksgiving

2:10 P.M.

"I'm just saying, dear, that I've never seen your mom so pale," Grandma Penny flicked the gravy ladle in the large vat of tan, globby liquid. Drips spattered onto the white lacy tablecloth they'd spread onto the ping pong table. "Even though Ohio doesn't get a whole lot of sun, she looks like the shade of slate. *I* even have more vibrant skin."

Wrinkles crinkled in the corners of Grandma's eyes.

Debatable, for sure, but when Charity glanced back at her mother who was hunched on the couch, her throat dried. Even mom's firebird hair had sprouted gray roots. She hadn't noticed this until shafts of light from the rectangular windows highlighted the colorless patches.

Grandma hunched over a wicker basket of rolls. Folds of her navy dress caught on a puddle from a green bean spill that had happened moments before. She hmphed and straddled her hips with her hands.

"Some help your cousins are being, making their poor old grandma get all the dishes onto this table. I'm writing them all out of the will, I've decided it."

Grandma brushed some cracker shards off a flower pattern on her stomach. Crumbs still resided in her translucent gray hair piled atop her head like sheep wool. But Charity decided not to mention anything.

She'll probably treat me like I'm stupid if I do. She always does.

"I'm even more surprised that you haven't been your usual, helpful self. No doubt your mother is rubbing off on you. Now." She gestured to the basement kitchen. Clusters of uncles and relatives who Charity had never met in her life, chatted over cucumber and dip, and cheese trays. "Go to the kitchen and get my world-famous cranberry sauce. Put it right here."

Two fingers tapped a non-stained spot on the lacy table-cloth. A miracle considering holes and other brown splotches had formed on most sections of the fabric.

Charity pressed her fingers together and interlocked them.

Curses curses curses.

Speaking of, she wondered how Io's family got along this Thanksgiving. Did they set a place at the table for her and hope she walked through the door and said, "Surprise! I wasn't really gone."

Grandma's tsk of her tongue drew Charity back to the present. Hand perched on her hip, she was waiting for an answer.

"Oh, Grandma, I don't know if that's the best idea."

"Tush. Do it, or I'll write you out of the will."

It was always so hard to tell if Grandma joked or meant

with all her heart about removing relatives from the Last Will and Testament of Penelope Hingerbogger. She threatened at least five times per family gathering to remove someone from the document that contained her last wishes.

Uncle Nestor forgot to bring the baked beans for the Fourth of July gathering. Goner.

Aunt Calypso didn't compliment Grandma's new Christmas outfit. RIP.

Mom breathed too loudly. Outta there.

Charity bobbled on her ankles. "You mean, I'm actually *in* the will?" Grandma had never threatened to remove her before, so she assumed she never existed in the document in the first place.

"Certainly. Someone needs to take my ball of yarn collection off my hands. Now, cranberry me."

Yarn skeins in peril of being forsaken forever, or thrown at some ungrateful cat, prodded Charity to bustle toward the kitchen. She did her best to weave around the cheese-eating uncles and wished Grandma hadn't made her take off the gloves when she arrived.

Thanksgiving
2:13 P.M.

Cranberry sauce splattered Charity's unicorn onesie. As though the fair young mythical creature had been gored in a great battle, so gleamed the wound in the warm basement light at her aunt's house.

Silence crashed over the room. The mere excitement

from a football commentator hummed from the television stationed over a fake-stone fireplace.

Eyes burned into the mess on Charity's outfit. It was the clown costume and ramen noodle girl all over again.

Her stomach churned as the scents of green beans and gravy wafted behind her. Worst of all, she smelled the creamed corn. The scent made her want to vomit.

Toes dug into the thick shaggy carpet. Her eyes roamed the room for anything but a puce face or lip sagged so deep into a frown, it almost trailed right off their chins.

She landed on her mother's ashen hands. Blank expression.

Cotton had filled her throat when she swallowed.

Shoulda grabbed Uncle Nestor's lukewarm cinnamon cider when I got the chance.

No wonder Mom hated family gatherings.

Thanksgiving

2:13 P.M. (and 20 seconds)

Charity set the glass bowl onto the table and observed the casualties. A mere sludge of cranberry and raisins remained at the bottom of the bowl. The rest had dyed her stomach. Chills ran down her legs as the sediment crawled onto the shaggy carpet.

She hadn't meant to trip on her aunt's tabby cat 'Tabby' on the way over to the ping pong table. Nor did she mean for the hood of her onesie to obscure her line of vision on the ten-foot journey.

But now, dripping red and reeking of tartness, she scanned the crowd once again for a friendly face. She landed on her mother's. And hoped the gray could disappear once more. Like it had back in the kitchen for a spare moment.

Nothing shifted.

Her gaze flicked over to her grandmother who brushed cranberry shrapnel off the flower on her dress.

"My dear. Can't you do anything right?"

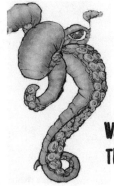

Chapter 25

Would've Brought A Rotisserie to Thanksgiving, Just to Watch the World Burn. . . .

Why are you upside down, Chair?"

"Seeing how long it takes all the blood in my body to flow to my head. It'll get heavy, and then explode. You, sir, are lucky enough to bear witness to this monumentous event."

Brightness from the phone illuminated Stefan's smirk. He rubbed his thumb against the corner of his lips to drain the excess turkey grease, somehow super visible on their video call.

"Well, if it helps, Chair, my family's Thanksgiving didn't go all that much better. Mom had volunteered to make the turkey, but with her lying around the house all the time, she forgot to get one at the store in time." He shuddered. "Don't ever try to replace a Thanksgiving turkey with a rotisserie chicken. There will be fights, drinks splashed into one another's faces, bite marks on arms, and an impromptu trip to the hospital when the arms don't stop bleeding."

He paused and dug his nail into his teeth.

"Hypothetically."

"I wonder why your mom lost motivation all of a sudden." Dark film-coated Charity's eyes and her head started to throb.

OK, body, fine. Since you won't make this explosion easy, we'll just have to hold off on the fireworks today.

She rolled onto her stomach, chin perched on her squid stuffed animal Inkheart. "Grandma wouldn't stop talking about how my mom's gotten all lazy, after she didn't help clean up the cranberry mess. Said she wished the sauce had spilled on Mom instead of me, so we can juice up that sickly gray skin."

Stefan shot up and banged his forehead against his bunk bed. He groaned, massaged his scalp, and slid onto his floor.

"Wait a sec, Chair, your family was talking about gray skin, too?"

"I mean, we live in Ohio. Clouds are gray, people are gray, no wonder our football teams wear orange and brown, to liven it up."

"No, I mean, my family was talking about how my Mom needs to go to Cancun to get a tan. You don't think the curse turns people into monochrome monsters, do you?"

She hmmed and dug her chin further into the cap of the neon green squid. "Do you mean, like the graffiti at the park turned gray when I touched it?"

"Or the book you found at the shop with the splotched spine."

Charity sighed, snatched her coat off the floor, and dug

into the pocket. Out she pulled the gray die from the park, the last gift Io had given her. Granted, Io didn't technically own the thing in the first place, but sentimentality knew no bounds.

"Chair, something about physical contact with humans and the curse turns things dull. Mom didn't get all mopey until Io brushed hands with her in the car. And you—well, you do like to give hugs. You're basically a curse's dream host."

Heat prickled her cheeks.

I'm definitely the curse's dumbest host, too.

She tugged at her hair until strands fell into her palms.

Pulses throbbed in her neck, either from the upside-down excursion from a moment ago or (the horror) from a realization. How often had she hugged her mom? Nestled her head onto her mom's neck during their Saturday movie nights?

"B-but," her voice shook, "I thought the curse was if we touched anything, especially when doing something kind, it would backfire. Not turn gray."

"True. But maybe that's just part of it. Like a Level One. We might be onto Level Two now. Kind of like King Midas, anything you touch turns to gold. Or in our case, a gray sad monster."

She stared at her palms and expected fireballs to burst from her skin.

Chapter 26

Could've Taken Up the Hottest Instrument
Since the Lyre. . . .

Hector's car rolled up her driveway, tires spraying gravel, and Paris popped his head out of the front seat window. He waved a leftover candy bar from Halloween. Her legs tugged her toward the maroon vehicle.

I know Mom says not to accept candy from strangers, but she never specified Halloween candy.

She snatched the chocolate bar and yanked open the sliding door for the back seat.

With a dive into a leather chair, she plugged her seatbelt and unwrapped the treat at the same time. An impressive feat if either of the two boys had de-cided to look at her in the rearview mirror. She popped a candy square into her mouth and crunched on the rice texture of the bar.

Paris curved around the front seat not to stare, alas, at her generous multi-tasking skills. Rather he appeared fixated on her sweater.

"Is that a dinosaur head sewn onto the front?"

She puffed out her chest so the T-Rex could get a bite of the front seat. Instead, the dinosaur 'chomped' on some papers stuffed into the seat pouch. Looked like game notes or something to do with a 'campaign.' She recalled Danae mentioning that Paris's brother liked all things Hoplites. "Found it at the thrift store. You did say to wear an ugly Christmas sweater."

"Why's it holding a menorah in its mouth?"

"I don't presume to know the religion of the dinosaurs. Now, why are you wearing a blah blue t-shirt?"

"I said we're going to see ugly Christmas *trees.*"

"And by saying so, you inferred we should wear sweaters to match."

Hector's eyelids squinched in the rearview mirror. "Paris, is she being serious?"

"Don't ask. I don't think any of us want to know."

Paris rolled his eyes and faced the road. Hector swerved around a group of female joggers bundled in scarves and neon leggings. He swung up the arm of his turn signal, and their car approached downtown.

Hector cleared his throat and turned down the volume of a whiny boy band on the radio.

"You ever been to the Ugly Christmas Tree Show Downtown, Charity?"

"What is the Ugly Christmas Tree Show Downtown?"

Blue Christmas - The Ugly Christmas Tree Show

Downtown

/my-hands-hurt-from-typing-so-many-pronunca-tions-send-help-get-me-fired!/

Noun.

1. Held in the Almsgiving Community Players building, a place where people put on local plays and the occasional school spelling bee, town members decorate trees as terribly as possible and put them up for auction. All proceeds went to the local children's hospital.

2. An event where school bands showed their prowess by playing the latest hip jams like "Carol of the Bells" and "All I Want for Christmas is You" on stage while folks perused the trees.

3. Incidentally, this happened to be the thirteenth year they held this event.

"Oooh that sounds lovely," she said. "I'd love to count how many times people crack their voices on high notes. There's something so beautiful about messing up."

This reminded her of the choir concert back in seventh grade with Io. She bet Io would've really loved this too.

Her foot crunched on a fast food bag bunched in the back seat. Seats, windows, everything smelled of old fries.

Paris and his brother exchanged a glance.

"Told you she's weirder than you, Hector."

"I know, I'm jealous."

"Jealous?"

"At least she has *personality*. The only interesting thing you do is learn the lyrics to Disney songs and sing them in the shower when you think no one is home."

"Do not."

This came out low and husky, almost a whimper. Paris Lightyear punched Hector in the arm—ignoring all driving safety precautions—and shrunk into his seat until his body disappeared from Charity's view. She'd always read him as a shy kid, but no wonder. Charity never had siblings, but she imagined they couldn't handle her Charity-ness if they had existed.

And with Danae's strong personality, made sense why Paris didn't get more than a few words out at a time.

A sniff sounded from Paris's seat. Either from the cold weather or the clearly emotional moment of his shameful Disney-reciting hobby being unearthed.

"Hec, why don't you show her the reason why we're looking at ugly trees in the first place?"

"Gladly. Under your seat, you'll find—"

Her heart vaulted in her throat for this pure Oprah moment.

"—a plastic water bottle. Do hand that up here. It's making a lot of noise."

That could explain the crunch she'd heard whenever they skidded to a halt at a stoplight. She grunted and managed to grip the grooves with her gloves. A sticky residue clung to the fabric when she handed him the bottle from behind.

"Thank you. And to your left, you'll find a tablet with a newspaper clipping that gave us our first clue about madam Cassandra. Borrowed it from the library database."

Lo, a shiny black screen with a thirteen-sided die pattern on the red sleeve glimmered in the light from the tinted windows. A tangerine sun peeked through the slate-gray clouds that covered Ohio in an everlasting winter cloak.

She scooped the device into her hands and de-gloved her fingertips for a long enough moment to open it. Here was to hoping the battery wouldn't disintegrate immediately.

Already open, a newspaper clipping stung her eyes from the bright glow. She squinted at the faint black letters.

"Wowser, you're right. I sure hope Mr. Pietz managed to find whoever egged his house."

"What?" Hector almost slammed into a car which braked suddenly. "No, those are the police listings. Go to the article on the right."

She pinched the writing to enlarge the letters and read:

Ringing Up the Right Tree: Local Handbells
Group Organizes Town-wide Charity Event
By HOLLY BELL

You may have heard of the latest trend, ugly
Christmas sweater parties. But a new "ugly"
trend has arrived downtown, and it's putting
the good in good cheer.

Local handbell group "Put a Ring on It" organized a charity event at the Almsgiving Community Players building. Suggested by group member and teenager Cassandra Agnes, the musicians have enlisted the help of stores, religious groups, and schools to contribute the most heinously decorated trees for charity.

"The idea was simple," Agnes said. "We take something ugly and turn it into something beautiful. Ugly trees are up for auction, and all donations will go to the Almsgiving Children's Hospital."

Held this Friday through December 12, members of the community are encouraged to–

To what? She never found out. Charity clicked the button on the side of the tablet, and the screen faded into darkness. They'd arrived at their destination.

Chapter 27

Would've Made a Garbage Tree if There Was More Time....

She stared out the windshield and watched Hector roll into a tight parking spot in between two large, gray cars. Folks wrapped in scarves and coats had their arms weighed down by large plastic bags with "Black Friday Sale" printed on them.

"The library didn't have anything else on Cassandra." Hector warmed his fingers on the blasting heaters up front. "But since the Christmas tree event starts today, and those handbell ringers usually kick off the event, we might have a chance to talk with them and find out what happened to her."

"*If* any of the members are still the same. It did happen thirteen years ago," Paris pointed out.

Sideways enough, Charity caught a glimpse of Paris's arms crossing his chest. He then un-pretzeled them and dug his arms into a winter coat he'd parked in his seat.

"Event starts in a few minutes," Hector said, "and I fig-ured we'd get here before the Black Friday sales crowd does." Hector unplugged the keys from the ignition and fiddled with strings on his scarlet red winter cloak.

Maybe there are other weirdos like you, Charity. He can wear a cloak in public, no problem.

She hoped that by the time she reached her high school years, she'd have infinite confidence.

They exited the car and found themselves in a winding line outside of a brick building. A man stationed up front in a peacoat swung open the doors for them. Warmth and bell music stung her ears upon entry.

The theater, similar to a high school gym, had bleachers flanking each of the two sides. Probably because before thes-pians used the building, the local rec volleyball team did. But they'd retracted the bleachers now.

Center stage, in the middle of the room, handbell play-ers in bright blue polos and black slacks rung silver-glinted bells. Butterly lights overhead caught on the bell lips. Garishly illuminated candy canes and blow-up Santas hung and deco-rated whatever the trees didn't in the hall. A distinct whiff of peppermint and hot chocolate wafted from a drinks station at the other end of the room.

She reached out and felt the fake bristle of a black spray-painted tree. Even underneath the gloves, the branches tickled her fingertips.

Ugly trees obscured the brick walls, and the three of them wandered to the right, following yellow arrows to indicate the pathway for sightseers.

Ah, I'm at home.

She imagined how Io would've giggled with her about the various trees and made her pose by them while they snapped funny photos.

"They'll probably ring a few more songs before they bring another group in to play." Paris shoved his hands into his pants pockets. "Might as well take a look at the trees."

As though they had a choice in the matter. The line behind them surged like water attempting to escape a clogged pipe. Almsgiving residents had an odd habit of falling in love with the irregular—all except for the inhabitants of the middle school. Perhaps, by the time Charity reached adulthood, she could at last fit in this place completely.

They continued down the aisle and observed the grotesque ornamentations.

A mid-sized tree caught her eye first with fast food wrapper baubles brimming over the edges. 'Put a Ring on It' began a chorus of "Jingle Bells," and Charity bounced along to the rhythm. She glanced over her shoulder and watched those with the biggest instruments plunk mallets on their bells.

They made a fun "thunk" noise.

The next contestant in the Miss Ugly Christmas Tree pageant was simply a pointy cardboard pyramid covered in black trash bags. A little wooden sign next to it indicated the starting auction price for the tree: $650.

A tree with chain mail and flails five contestants down caught Hector's eye and he bustled over to it. Beside Charity,

Paris moaned through his nostrils.

"Don't worry, Paris, I doubt he could afford that. His payment via cafeteria snacks seems in no way sustainable."

"It's not that . . . it's just." He sighed and rubbed his thumb up and down absently on an evil clown ornament on a haunted circus-themed tree, complete with a circus tent star. "It's hard enough having a curse and losing all my friends on the cross country team. But with a brother like him, it's surprising I had any friends in the first place."

He sniffed—

Someone get this poor kid a Kleenex or allergy meds.

—and returned his wayward hand back into his pocket.

"I mean, he has those stupid Hoplite campaigns at my house all the time. Even before the curse, it would be nice to invite some guys over to play video games. But not with Hector and his friends in togas and throwing foam daggers at each other."

Charity bopped with excitement when the handbell group broke out some wooden sticks and rubbed them on the bells in a circular motion. It made the notes sound like they were floating underwater. Memories of the eee from the lake filled her ears for a moment.

Every eee shifted to an eye sound, like Io. Energy surged into her veins afresh when she thought of her friend, and why she needed to find answers to save her.

"You know, maybe those friends weren't worth keeping. If they can't handle a man in a toga, how will they ever survive college . . . or a true friendship?"

She thought back to the girls on the basketball team, about how no one would put their clothes in a locker near hers. About how they would get silent anytime Charity entered a room.

With a pluck and a slam against the foam on the clothed tables, the ringers ceased their song, and pulled Charity back to the present. The ringers hunched over and pulled out thick black suitcases to house the bells. Charity perked up at the silence and gestured at Hector to move toward the tables.

Go time.

They weaved through the clumped crowd and dodged legs, arms, and a lack of ugly sweaters until they reached the handbell tables. It could've been Charity's imagination, but she thought she spotted the unmistakable raven braid in the shuffle.

Danae?

No time to double-check. She had some investigating to do.

Hector puffed out one breath and then waved to get the attention of a woman with short curly hair and glasses. "Milady, you performed excellently." He bowed and rolled his wrist in a flourish.

"Umm, thanks." On her polo, she had the name "Bella" stitched in black cursive font.

"Would you happen to know anyone in this engaging ensemble who has performed at this venue since the first event?"

She wiped the back of her forehead with a black glove.

Charity had noticed they performed without using their bare hands. Probably to prevent hand oils from getting on the bells . . . or erasing fingerprint evidence if they killed someone with the instruments. A tossup.

"Oooh, boy." Bella frowned. "I guess I've been with the group the longest outta this bunch. But I joined the year after the first event."

"So, the director changed since then?"

Paris inserted this question before the other two could. Perhaps to feel important, or that he endured a ride in a fast-food scented car for something.

"Yeah, she quit about five years ago, but I did get to perform under her." She said this with a solemn hand fold and bow. Either the choir director had died, or worse, gone snow-birding in Georgia.

Light from a dangled candy cane overhead flashed red in Hector's eyes.

"Did your former director ever happen to mention a handbell player named Cassandra?"

Bella jolted back and knocked over a folder stand on the table behind her. She clutched at her chest with a fist.

"No, can't say that I have." Her voice shot up to a high-bell octave. She weaved her gloved fingers into her hair, but the cloth caught on a curl. Abandoning ship, she left the glove in a tangle and polished the bells on the table with a black cloth.

"Come on!" Paris slammed his hands on the table. But because the players had covered the surface in a foam pad, the sound muffled. "We got evidence at the library that she played with this group thirteen years ago. You joined a year after. You *had* to have heard something. And if my brother is going to show up in public in that ridiculous Red Riding Hood cloak, then you better make it worth it."

Wowza, Paris standing up to the man. Well, wo-man.

Not being under the scrutiny of Danae's glare had its wonders and benefits.

Unfazed, Bella started to shove bells into a case. "I don't know what you're talking about."

Hector pulled out his tablet—

Where on earth had he been keeping that?

—and the screen illuminated a scary-eager grin.

"Oh yeah, well take a look at—" his voice dropped, cracked, "this?"

Charity took two steps back and hoisted herself on her tiptoes to glance at the screen. The file had disappeared and a red "Error" replaced its slot. Had her touch back in the car eradicated the newspaper from the device?

Bella waved her hand at some invisible bug near her sharp nose. "Sorry, kids, but I don't have time for this. We need to pack up in the next five minutes before the 'Looking Sharp Jazz Choir' gets here." She jerked her chin over her shoulder at her other band members who hoisted suitcases full of bells onto rolling carts.

They needed to act, now.

When Bella turned to shove some mallets covered in yellow yarn into a black felt bag, Charity tore both gloves with

148

her teeth, spat them on the floor, and gripped the handle of a bell the size of a baby doll's head. Her arm swung down a few inches under its weight.

"What are you—" Bella stiffened. She sweetened her voice. "Now, put that thing down on the table. Nice and easy."

With a knee crack, Bella lunged forward for the bell. But Paris and Hector stepped in front of Charity to form a barricade. Blanched, Bella whirled around to call for the aid of her bell-mates, but they were busy grunting and heaving the carts toward the door.

Now, for the bad cop sans good cop routine Charity'd practiced with her stuffed animals. This would, in no way, make Bella's world a better place today. But she needed to do this for Io.

"I hate to do this, Bella, and I never envisioned myself being a CIA interrogator. That was twenty-seventh on my list of possible occupations for me in the future, next to skydiving instructor and corgi herder. But you've left me with no choice."

"Listen, do you want money?" She dug a leather wallet out of her black slacks, opened it, and waved a neon-orange business card. "I have a coupon for two dollars off a pint of ice cream at The Scoop. You want?"

Oooh, ice cream.

Memories of sweet pralines of butter pecan mixed with cotton candy swirled over her tongue. Her favorite combo.

No, focus.

"Ma'am, if you do not tell us what you know about Cassandra, I'm afraid I'll have to . . . have to," she made a claw with her fingers. Digits wriggled like spider legs, "have to touch this bell with my bare hands."

Bella slapped both palms against her over-blushed cheeks. She gasped.

Charity's fingers squirmed so much, aches formed in her palms. She'd never threatened anyone before. Hoped she wouldn't have to again. But for Io . . . she'd even get a finger-print on this bell.

"Think of the oils from my skin." She slithered each s like a snake. "The tarnish on this beauty. Bet it will take forev-er to wipe off. What is this?" Her thumb budged down an inch to reveal the label on the black handle. "A middle C."

"Yes." Bella's voice tremored. She even crunched two crooked teeth down onto her pink lipsticked bottom lip.

"That's an important note, isn't it?"

"Some would argue that it's the bread and butter that holds the music together."

"Pity if I touched it . . . or even worse. Dropped it."

Her fingers wriggled closer, closer . . . a centimeter away . . . .

"Wait!"

Charity let both arms go slack. The bell rested against the fabric of her pants.

"Yes?" Relief flooded her.

Knees a-wobble, Bella whipped her head over each shoulder. The only other member of her group still left in the room was busy collapsing a table. She turned back to them and hunched in. Flowery perfume overwhelmed Charity's nostrils to the point where they stung.

"I don't know a whole lot. Our old handbell director didn't like to talk about Cassandra much. But—"

She bristled as Charity's fingers closed in on the bell's bowl.

"—I do know that something went awry during the first Ugly Christmas Tree show. Something that involved Cassandra."

Charity's breath hitched.

Paris found enough oxygen to get out the words she couldn't. "What happened?"

"Don't know exactly. The newspapers had already covered this event and didn't want to devote much more page space to it. Plus, it's not exactly newsworthy to say, 'Woman yells at thirteen-year-old girl,' and some debacle about a house getting egged took up the front page the next week anyway."

Stupid Mr. Pietz. Couldn't avoid hogging the spotlight for one week, now could you?

"But I do know some woman confronted her during this event. Something about an accident that happened in Semele Park. That's all I know."

Charity scanned the watery eyes of the woman for two Mississippi's before she placed the bell on the table. The three of them shuffled away as Bella put the last bell into her suitcase and slammed the lid shut.

Here was hoping that the handle wouldn't break off because Charity touched it with her bare fingertips.

They wavered by the trash bag pyramid tree as a crowd clump filtered past them.

"That was amazing, madame Charity," Hector nodded at her. If he wore a top hat, she imagined he would've tipped the brim at her.

"Yeah, seriously, you had me scared." Paris shoved his hands into his pockets. "Remind me never to make you mad. Like, ever."

Heat blossomed in Charity's cheeks. She wished she could use her Menorah-eating dinosaur to hide her grin.

"Well, since we seem to have another clue, maybe we should go check out the library?" Paris suggested. "They might have a newspaper clipping about a park accident."

Hector ruffled his cape to get a piece of fuzz off the hem. "No can do, bro. Charity paid me for one adventure only. We got an answer to her research question. Actually driving her to this event came gratis. Good thing I like ugly Christmas trees." He winked.

She dug a fist into her pocket and pulled out a wadded five dollars she'd found behind her bookshelf after the Thanksgiving incident.

"If we stop by a store, I could get you some candy bars."

He patted an ample stomach pouch. "Got plenty of sweets at Thanksgiving, thank you. Dad went crazy with the marshmallows on the sweet potato casserole this year. And besides, even if I hadn't, five dollars isn't going to get you far in an adventure."

What are the inflation rates of adventures?

"Bro, it's to end a curse for me and her. Don't you want to help your family out?" Paris flicked a piece of his hair back with a neck jerk. The strand got caught on a false teeth ornament.

"The curse makes you *interesting*, though, bro. So mopey and mysterious. Girls like that, you know."

Hector must have had dozens of girlfriends by this point. No doubt he wooed them with his Lord of the Rings replica necklace he had on the floor of his backseat. He rubbed his chin with his thumb and smirked. "Although, I could be persuaded to go on another adventure if the kind madame can do me a favor first."

Paris's jaw sank in what Charity could only guess was a protest. Or because his mandibles wanted some exercise.

She tucked a tangle braid behind her ear and spoke. "What did you have in mind?"

Chapter 28

Should've Gone Rogue. . . .

R emind me again why you had Dad drop us off at your friend's house in togas?"

Stefan shivered at the base of the driveway as his father's car skittered past. His dad had spent the whole drive talking about how he liked to hit the tennis ball at his opponent's ankles. Tires kicked up icy slush onto their feet. Didn't help that Hector insisted they go as historically accurate as possible, and they wore brown leather sandals.

Charity had to paint her's brown. Pink glitter still poked through the acrylics she'd dug up in the basement storage closet.

"Hector said if I did a campaign of Hoplites with him today he'd help me dig up the next clue. I guess he's a player short. One got a concussion from whacking herself in the forehead with the hilt of a replica Celtic knight sword. And he mentioned something about today being a LAD day."

LAD

/lad-or-as-the-Scotts-say-laddie/

Noun

1. Live Action Dress-up (L.A.D.). Dress up as characters from Delphonian Hoplites and get ready to
impale each other with fake weapons.

2. That's it. Not everything needs to have two
definitions, you know. Take that, teachers who
always made me outline using at least two numbers
per point.

"Right." Stefan kicked a stone and the rock landed on
a patch of wet, brown grass. Most of the snow had melted,
leaving behind dead yards full of mini lakes. "I meant why did
you make *me* come along?"

"You said you died in the other campaign. That was awfully rude of them to kill you off."

"That's the point of the game. To kill people off. And
I was going to re-spawn as a mason, I'll have you know." He
shook his head, which either had dandruff or snow on his
hairs. "But Io is worth it."

Indeed.

She traced the lines up the driveway with her sandals.
Resilient dandelions sprouted in cracks and on the edge of
the brittle grass, despite the cold. One more snowstorm could
obliterate them.

"Chair, you do know how to play Delphonian Hoplites,
right?"

They approached the doorstep and she grinned at a large wreath hung on the red door. Sure it didn't have any flails or trash bags hanging from it, but the fake holly and frosted pine cones served as a decent substitute.

Stefan tripped on the soles of his sandals and rang the doorbell. "Chair?"

"I mean you avoid getting killed, right? Do I need to know anything else?"

His facial features sagged. The door swung inward a moment later. An autumn patterned laurel wreath decorated Hector's ears. The orange and yellow leaves reminded Charity of a table decoration back at her aunt's house.

"Welcome to my humble abode. Oh," he backed into a wooden, windy banister, "you brought a guest."

"Figured he could walk me through the ropes. Since I'm filling in for a person and all, it would be rude for me to die for her."

Hector scratched his neck. "Might take some adjusting of plans, but if you have a ready-made character, that could make it easier."

Stefan puffed out his chest.

"Sure do. Class seven, shield-bearer." He patted a gold-painted circular shield hoisted on his arm. A sun pattern indented the cheap plastic material.

Stefan's voice had shot up to a 'Hi, I just swallowed helium from a balloon' level. That meant he'd lied.

In either case, Hector's fuzzy-wuzzy eyebrows vaulted into his forehead for a moment. "Well," he clapped his palms and then motioned for them to enter, "I guess you'll have no problem jumping right into the game. Larisa's a class six mystic, so that's a lot for a beginner to have to take on. If you kill off her character today, she'll find a way to bonk you on the head with a Celtic sword."

Charity tried to decide if that was a threat or a promise. A Celtic indent in one's forehead could form a cool pattern.

Their shoes squeaked on the hardwood floor. Stefan shut the door behind them, and they followed Hector down a skinny hallway. A room to the left housed a piano and a two-stringed oval-shaped instrument.

"We're going to get started with the LAD-ing soon, so meet us downstairs." He gestured to a rectangular archway on the right. Golden lights followed white steps down, which wound and disappeared.

"In the meantime, Dad set up some snacks. Leftovers from Thanksgiving. Fill up, come down, and," a glint flashed in his pupils, "don't die."

He disappeared down the steps and they found themselves at a copper kitchen table with plates of Hors d'oeuvres.

Charity grabbed a black olive and popped it into her mouth. Briny juices exploded.

Not bad, with a slab of Nutella, this bad boy would be golden.

A tall man with a tennis band around his forehead appeared from a nearby bedroom. He waved. "You kids have fun at the campaign, all right?"

Stefan and Charity nodded at who Charity presumed

was Paris and Hector's dad. The supposed father paused near the front door. "Any chance either of you like sweet potato casserole?" He checked his watch and nearly jolted. "Sorry, got to wallop some guy who thinks it's funny to aim at his opponent's sneakers. Please feel free to dish yourself some casserole in Tupperware."

With that, he disappeared. Stefan's dad he no idea the reckoning he'd have to deal with.

"OK, game plan." Stefan snapped a cracker with his tooth. Sawdust sprinkled onto the blue Persian rug next to the table. "We need to give you a boot camp on how to survive a campaign of Hoplites without dying."

"Cool, cool. Mind if we write it down on a list?" She reached for a napkin and a pen on the table.

"Umm, sure, why?"

"I like lists. I even have a list for the reasons I like lists, but I don't know if we're close enough, Stefan, for me to show you that."

"Fine."

1. Every man, woman, and other mythical creature for themselves.

2. Attack the weakest link.

3. Be stoic. Poker face, but please save poking actual faces for when you engage in attack mode.

4. Have fun. But not too much fun (glares).

"Happy?"

"Thank you."

She popped another olive into her mouth and flew down the staircase. When she hit the landing, she observed gray.

That is, someone had draped gray sheets over the walls and similar-hued tissue paper over the lights. No wonder Paris had to wear a Buzz Lightyear sheet to initiation. Hector had stolen all the other muted color sheets for his setup down here. She thought back to Semele park and how everything there had also felt very un-Almsgiving.

No furniture showed its face, if furniture had a face to show, anywhere. She guessed the sheets might have draped over a couch or chair if she scrutinized them closely enough. They did seem to billow a few feet off the walls.

A smoky-scented candle flickered on a stool.

"Welcome," Hector said, "mystic and shield-bearer, we're about to begin."

Charity grinned at the group, but moments later her lips shifted to a thin straight line. All clad in togas, shields, and various spray-painted foam blades, the group shared a collective scowl.

Oh right, poker face. Had to get tough.

Think gritty thoughts, Charity. Nails, chainsaws, garden gnomes. That's it.

Her eyebrows slanted so much they squeezed the bridge of her nose. Hector squinched his eyelids, either confused or in desperate need to use the restroom soon.

"All right, you all know the rules—"

On top of his white toga, a navy sheet draped around his

159

shoulder and sagged onto his arm.

"—but as town philosopher, I'm required to give a brief overview for each campaign. Welcome to the city of Delphos. Here, the warriors are tougher than Spartans, smarter than Athenians, and most importantly, we look out for ourselves and our survival."

Cobwebs glimmered in the corner of the room. Charity hoped she could meet the spider friend who had gone missing from the silky strands.

"Show weakness, and you choose death. Each player gets a turn, and because we're doing a LAD day, once everyone has a turn, we get to battle it out in the arena."

He gestured to a carpeted platform at the other end of the room. Dance mirrors reflected spiky dangled lights overhead the stage.

What a basement!

"Now that the rules have been established, let's begin our story." His voice drained of all color. Perhaps his vocal cords had to put on a poker face too. "Last week we left off with our resident mystic," he gestured at Charity, "setting fire to the town library. This puts her in the lead, and our librarian," he jabbed a finger at a girl with long legs and static electricity hair, "slash town poet considerably injured and weakened and her library in near-shambles."

The curls reminded Charity of Io, except instead of dark mahogany, they were electric blue. Sadness squeezed her chest. She let it linger for a moment until it shifted into a fire.

Keep playing the game. We need to save Io.

Librarian chick spun a sword in her fingertips. Moments later, the hilt flung out of control toward the gray curtain. A corner of the sheet popped off the clothespin hanging it to a string, and scarlet paint peeked out from underneath.

Like the crimson scar on the monkey bars in the park.

"Because we have a new civilian in our midst, a shield-bearer, no less, he has the first turn before our mystic, who is in the lead, goes. Shield-bearer, what is your first move?"

Stefan turned to the side, lips pursed. He snapped his fingers.

"I search the town for Greek fire to finish the job on the library."

Yikes, she knew he had some late fees on movies he'd borrowed from their local library branch, but Stefan went hardcore.

"Please roll, then, shield-bearer."

He dug into his sweatpants pockets. Both of them decided to wear some form of pantaloons underneath their togas. Not historically accurate, but at least their sandals were brown.

Bright orange, the translucent die glimmered in his fingertips. He tossed the triskaidecagon—

OK, so maybe Charity researched the name of a thirteen-sided 3-D object one day in study hall and was *dying* for an occasion to use the word.

—object and on the short carpet, the number nine gleamed.

"Congrats, you rolled relatively high."

Cool, so I guess rolling a high number is a good thing in this game.

"You locate a town salesman who is selling Greek fire, but he charges you a great deal for it. You don't have enough drachma, but if you sell one of your weapons, you can purchase the fire. We'll hear your decision during your next roll."

Rolls, sushi rolls sounded nice right now.

Could go with those olives and Nutella.

"Now, mystic."

Charity snapped, legs and spine straight.

Soldier ready to comply, sir!

"Since you have the lead, you begin the next turn. What will your move be?"

Hmm, Stefan took the pyromaniac decision away. And even if she wanted to burn a library down—

Hahahahahahaha no, never. Those poor, poor books!

—-redundancy was practically a sin. They left her with one choice.

"Nothing."

Hector blinked. "Umm, mystic who has incredible powers of healing allies, destruction of buildings via the conjuring of Greek fire, and feasibly anything but the ability to heal yourself choose to do . . . nothing?"

"Yup." Her cheeks burned.

Did I choose wrong, again?

She checked her outfit and remembered she was wearing a toga and not a clown suit.

The others in the group let their poker faces slip. One boy even shot his eyebrows so high, they disappeared into his long, floppy hair. Another girl, mid-swallow from a water bottle, choked on the liquid. She coughed and muttered something about a "wrong pipe."

Charity dug into the pockets of her sweats and pulled out the gray die from the park. Her Uncle Ricky, who enjoyed the Rocksino Casino up in Cleveland, mentioned at family gatherings how he'd like to blow on the dice before chucking them at a green table. Sage advice from her elder in mind, she puffed onto the die.

So much so, that spit flew out of her mouth and propelled the triskaidecagon onto the carpet. She leaned over to catch the number.

One.

"Mystic, you rolled an unfortunate number. Because you decided to take the day off and do nothing, a group of barbarians rolled in and destroyed your apothecary and left you wounded. You are now operating at fifty percent capacity. We'll hear about your decision next roll," he dropped his voice low, "which hopefully will involve doing *something*."

Call her crazy, but she didn't remember barbarians existing at the same time as the Greeks in her Jr. High Ancient History class. How much research had the creator of this game put into the particulars? Or did the narrator, Hector, decide what happened in this campaign?

Everyone in the circle went around and took turns. Most of their moves involved trying to buy the Greek fire from the merchant to burn the library, stabbing the librarian, and trying to give Cerebrus, the three-headed dog of the Underworld, a belly rub without getting decapitated.

Once they all had a turn, Hector had them break off to do LAD combat.

Charity motioned for Stefan to converse with her off to the side. Everyone else advanced to the stage platform. Players wiggled their fingers like centipede legs and whacked at each other with foam swords.

"It doesn't matter if we miss this part, right?" She blew a small braid off her nose.

"Nah, it's just giving our resident philosopher time to think of what happens next. Nothing that happens during physical LADing has any effect on the game."

Sure enough, Hector had dodged to the side, where a gray pillar left him in a shadow. He was muttering. She caught spare words like "Gorgon," "Sphinx," and "Regicidal Yo-Yos."

She watched over her shoulder as three players circled in on the librarian with their shields. The girl cowered, as best she could with those spindly legs.

"Stef, why's everyone going after her? I mean, is it because they're jealous of her blue hair?"

Stefan frowned at a dent in his plastic shield. One whiff too strong of Axe wafted from him. "It's because she's the weakest link. Everyone else is at fifty percent health capacity or greater. She's at five percent. One more light blow, and we can finish her off."

Heaviness tugged at Charity's chest like it had back at

the park. This reminded her of when her father left. In a way, it felt like he, too, had 'finished her off' to get the wife he really wanted.

Chewing on some loose skin on her lip, she pulled out the gray die again. White numbers rolled in her palms. Thunder jolted in her left ear, and she snapped to attention. Hector clapped his palms once more, and the group ceased their fake fighting and returned to the circle.

"After a great battle and another day," Hector said, "we resume our order in which we began. Shield-bearer, your next move?"

Stefan thrust his shield on the carpet.

It would've looked and sounded cooler if they'd created the weapon out of metal instead of cheap plastic.

"I sell my shield to get some extra drachma. So I can watch that library burn."

The librarian hung her neck. A pit dug its way into Charity's stomach. She tried to ignore it.

Don't do anything stupid, Chair.

She winced when she caught the librarian's pitiful lip-sagging expression.

Stefan dropped his die and rolled an eight, and managed to get some drachma, but the merchant also sneaked a baby hydra into his satchel, which ate his food provisions for the day.

"Mystic, your turn, what do you do?"

She crossed her ankles, uncrossed, crossed again. Eyes on the librarian. Could wipe out this girl in a second. Or worse, watch as the rest of those in the campaign do that, and do . . . nothing.

Wait a moment. Last round, when she did exactly nothing, Hector had pointed out all the things she actually could do: Heal allies, destroy buildings, do mystic stuff.

She'd choose one of those.

And I can still be myself, too, while doing it.

"I choose to heal the librarian."

Maybe she could make an ally. They'd knocked her down to fifty percent last round. If she helped the librarian, maybe . . . .

Lightning appeared to stiffen the shoulders and spines of everyone in the circle. The librarian's eyes widened so much, they made her holographic eyeshadow disappear.

"Umm, all righty, the mystic chooses to heal the librarian. Your roll."

Shoot. Her luck would probably roll low and poison the librarian with hemlock. This time, without blowing on the dice, she dropped the totem onto the carpet.

Thirteen.

"Mystic, your healing powers have restored the librarian to one hundred percent health, with no damage dealt to either of you. You will decide in your next turn where to go from here."

She beamed at the girl with blue hair. The other didn't return the expression.

Oh, right, poker face.

It was so hard to catch onto all the new rules. She battled the feeling of being thrust into an alternative world. Gray lights and draped sheets didn't help with the discombobulated sensation. Like she had in the park, back with Io. Where weights clung to her calves like barbells, and she wanted, more than anything, to take a nap.

Io . . . energy flooded Charity's veins. She needed to focus and stay awake to save her.

"All right," Hector said. "Craftsman, you're next."

CRAFTSMAN: I choose to throw my ceramics at the mystic and her apothecary.

SOLDIER: I choose to throw my spear at the mystic and her apothecary.

FARMER: I choose to throw my cow at the mystic and her apothecary.

Near the end of the round, everyone had brought Charity down to five percent life when most of the players rolled high. The only one, the farmer, who rolled a three, got mad cow disease instead. His cows, mad, trampled all over his crops.

They'd found the weak link. The girl who knew nothing about this game.

Shock, gasp, swoon.

At last, they'd reached the final roll before they'd duke it out on stage with the foam swords. The librarian's fiery eyes met Charity's, and hope bobbled in her throat, along with the salty aftertaste of the olives.

Would she make an ally at last? She'd healed the librarian after all.

The librarian snarled her upper lip. "I choose to throw a

scroll at the mystic and her apothecary."

Knowledge, that hurt the worst.

Charity's eyes stung from the prick of tears.

Gosh, it's dusty down here.

She clawed a scab on her arm and searched the Librarian's eyes for some hint of mischief or a 'just kidding, I want to lend her an entire scroll-shelf (did they have bookshelves back then?) for saving my life.'

The dark claws of the Big Sad squeezed her stomach.

The not kidding librarian pulled black die out of the folds of her pink toga and let the object plunk onto the carpet. She rolled a thirteen.

"A brutal blow is delivered to the mystic. Happening to be allergic to paper cuts, she suffered fatal wounds at the bombardment of scrolls being tossed through the broken windows of her shop."

And thus, Charity died thanks to the die.

Her arms crossed her chest so tightly that her shoulders concaved. "I saved your life." Charity's voice cracked.

"Ah," Hector raised a knowing finger, "but she was not your ally, nor did she intend to be. The *smart* decision would've been to kill her off."

Smart stung Charity's ears like a needle prick. "But-but, why would you kill someone who saved you?"

Hector clapped a hand on her shoulder, and his features softened. "Sorry, Charity, but in this game, niceness is weakness. And weakness gets you killed every time."

Chapter 29

Could've Committed Murder and Scrolled Through Insta at the Same Time. . . .

Gloves aren't going to make up for the fact you killed me."

Charity crossed her arms and legs on the soft family room couch upstairs until she formed a tightly wound pretzel. Next to her leg lay a Venus flytrap drawing she'd traced into the impressionable cushion fabric.

"Not *just* gloves," Hector waved the purple mitts like pom poms, "you can use tech with these." He tapped the gray fingertips, knit in a different fabric. "So when you touch my tablet, it won't erase the library files. I guess your curse does affect things like tech. Especially since you're being kind to Io and Cassandra by getting them un-kidnapped."

She scrunched her nose. "Library files?"

"Duh, so we can head to our next destination. Into Gringolet we go."

'Ccording to Stefan, Gringolet was some horse that showed up in an Arthurian story. And apparently an apt name for Hector's fry-scented car.

"You mean," she untucked her arms, hope buoying in her chest, "you found the next clue already?"

"Sure, dug it up yesterday. Figured you'd come here and kill off Larisa the mystic's character. A favor to everyone else, really. She'd let the polis run wild with centaurs."

So I guess my stupidity did help people out. Who knew?

Her bounce caused the cushion to groan underneath her. She halted. "Isn't Paris coming?" She scanned the banister that led upstairs. He hadn't popped his head out during the several-hour campaign.

"Said he had a Coalition meeting. I guess you technically had one too, but I was happy you chose to come here instead."

Shadows filled her chest. She'd never gotten a text about that. Had Danae arranged a meeting without letting her know?

Charity shoved herself off the couch and followed him to the driveway, after putting on the new techie gloves. Hector clicked open the front seat for her, gentleman style, and a number of fast food drink cups and napkins rolled out onto the pavement. In she went.

She grabbed the tablet and opened the first file.

Frown, lip sag toward the bacon-scented carpet.

"Umm, Hec, this first article mentions an accident at the playground, but there are no names listed. All we have is the date and that some thirteen-year-old bonked their forehead into the monkey bars. It doesn't even tell us if the victim's a he or she."

"Yeah," he plugged the key into the ignition. Gringolet groaned and chugged and roared, "most accidents like that

170

don't get too specific. Parents don't want names getting out. But you might want to click on the other file I'm borrowing from the local library. Mind you, one that wasn't destroyed by Greek fire."

She exited the one article and tapped the other. Off-white paper filled the screen. A pinch enlarged the image of a smiling girl. Even in the black and white photo, you could tell she had dark curly hair and sharp cheekbones.

Obituaries
Helen Tiresias, 13, of Almsgiving

Pause. Her throat dried, chest grew heavy. She glanced at Hector as he adjusted the rearview mirror. One corner had gone crooked.

"Hec, what is this?"

"You can read, can't ya?"

"Well, yes, but where are we going? There's nothing about Cassandra anywhere in any of these two articles."

"See, that's just the thing. The obituary is for October, a month before the charity Christmas tree event. I did a little digging on social media to see if Cass knew Helen. After all, it's a small town."

Silence filled the car, with the whir and whine of the engine.

"Well?" Charity asked.

"Turns out, they were best friends."

A weird feeling overtook Charity. Like someone had

dropped a bowling ball onto her stomach. She didn't like thinking about best friends and obituaries paired together. Time to shift the subject. "Are we visiting Helen's mom?"

"Nah, most of her relatives cleared out of town after her death. And those who stuck around moved recently. All of Cassandra's folks are gone, too. Most went to Florida. There's only one person left in drivable distance who's related to Helen." He flipped up his turn signal. "Her cousin Zoe."

Chapter 30

Should've Known Bubble Tea Isn't Actually Made of Bubbles, Bummer. . . .

When a woman with a buzzcut and septum ring answered the door, Charity fought the urge to hug her and call her 'best friend.'

Best friend peeked out behind a chain lock. "Can I help you?"

"Are you Zoe?" Hector's voice pricked Charity's ears in the cold.

"Yes?" Zoe scanned their bobbing legs. Charity tried her best not to jiggle her calves too much on that narrow stoop. Otherwise, she'd knock off the only decoration, a ceramic swan. "I'm assuming you're not the ones who are here to deliver my wings." She flashed her phone, open to a food delivery app. "They're an hour late."

Hector cleared his throat. "We were wondering if we'd be able to ask you some questions."

Zoe lifted her penciled on eyebrows. "About?"

Oh boy, I may not be the brightest, but from what I can remember from my therapy sessions with Stefan's mom, you have to approach this lightly. She's probably had oodles of people asking her about her cousin's death.

"We want to discuss your cousin's death," Hector said.

Wow Hector, way to ease her into the situation.

Wrinkles formed on Zoe's forehead and the corners of her eyelids in a wince. Like he'd punched her in the gut. "Sorry, kids, but even though that was thirteen years ago, I still don't feel comfortable—"

She began to shut the door.

"Wait," Charity's voice crackled in her throat, "please, we want to help. Your answers might be able to bring back a missing girl. Maybe more."

"Help." Zoe whispered the word. Her breath hitched and wisped away in a cloud of smoke. "Isn't that a funny word?"

With that, she shut the door.

Typical. I said the wrong thing, didn't I?

Then, something metallic jiggled inside, and seconds later, Zoe flung open the green door. "I made way too much bubble tea and need someone to drink it." She gestured them to head in with the sweep of an arm. "And," she paused, "it could be good to finally talk to someone about this. At least, someone who isn't a therapist."

They followed her inside, and Charity undid the straps on her sandals, an impressive feat in gloves, even techie ones.

She kicked off the shoes near a side table wrapped in a garland. Faint sweet potato scents floated from a kitchen nearby.

Barefoot and free, she let a shaggy hallway carpet tickle her soles all the way to a family room where Zoe perched on a blue leather chair.

Zoe, with a teacup in hand, gestured at the kitchen a room over.

"Pour yourself some tea and boba."

Milky liquid the shade of lavender sat in a pitcher next to a bowl of black tapioca pearls. Charity selected a teacup with a golden rim. After she plunked in a healthy number of pearls in her cup, she watched in delight as the purple liquid spilled over them like a river on rocks.

She sipped and a sweet creamy taste exploded on her tongue.

Hector trailed behind with a polka dot vessel. They both parked on a tan couch, angled toward the blue chair.

"So," Zoe lifted her glass to her lips, "what do you want to know?"

"We know she was friends with someone named Cassandra."

Zoe flinched when the name crossed Hector's lips. She dropped her shoulders, as though indicating he could continue.

"You were likely very young at the time," Charity put in, hoping Hector would get the hint to approach this more delicately.

"Ten," Zoe agreed.

"But do you remember anything about their friendship?" Charity asked.

With a hmm, Zoe crossed her ankles. At this moment, Charity realized Zoe was wearing neon green leggings.

"I do know that they were inseparable," Zoe said. "Helen didn't have a whole lot of friends, because Aunt Cya was . . ." She swirled her pearls in her cup with a wrist spin. "Was into really strange things."

"A witch?" Charity suggested. That could explain the curse part.

"No, not a lucrative occupation, I imagine." Zoe kicked out her legs onto an ottoman. Various magazines with photographs of dollars and men in suits perched her ankles. "She owned a game shop downtown until she left for Punta Gorda. Had a really good relationship with other local businesses. She and the bookstore would exchange books and games as gifts for the staff."

Game shop . . . did she mean *the* Ye Olde Pawn Shoppe?

"Woman loved creating games in her spare time. Would always try to get us to play her newest creation at family gatherings." Zoe sipped. "Anyway, I know that Cassandra always looked out for Helen. Because Cya was strange—"

As anyone who loves board games enough to create a business around them would be.

"—Helen drew a lot of attention from bullies."

Zoe's features darkened. She set her cup on a swan-shaped coaster and hugged one knee.

"I-I thought I could do this, but I'm not sure if I can."

She blinked a redness out of her eyes.

"Staying behind was hard enough when everyone else left town to forget. Well, if you can call, 'staying behind' moving back here after college." Sigh. "Granted, don't have to eat that awful orange marshmallow gelatin during the Fourth of July, since all the family gatherings happen in Florida."

Plan A for Charity: Move to Florida to avoid Gram-Gram's cranberry sauce and Aunt's weird creamed corn concoction.

Plan B: There is no plan B. Fleeing the state was the only option.

A refrigerator hummed in the silence. Charity tucked her feet into her knees, criss-cross applesauce, and siphoned a tapioca pearl into her mouth with her tongue.

"We don't have to talk about what happened at the park." Charity chewed on the sweet, squishy pearl. "Why don't we go back to your aunt? As the self-proclaimed, and classmate-proclaimed, weirdest person in my eighth-grade class, I'd love to know what made her strange."

Zoe squinted at a pair of pointe ballet slippers that hung on a nail on the wall above a TV cabinet. Then she snapped her fingers and rose from her spot.

"Aunt Cya always liked to go to the bookstore to hear from local authors, whenever they gave talks or signed books. Said it was a great way to hold crossover events over at her game store, and because Helen really liked to read. It helped her escape the kids in her class."

She jabbed a finger in the air and motioned it over the

spines of books on a shelf nestled between the TV cabinet and the wall.

"One local author in particular, who set her book in our hometown, got Cya's interest—ah ha!"

With the nudge of two fingers, she wedged out a book with a gray, matte spine. Aside from some yellowed pages, the unbent cover indicated Zoe hadn't read the book all that much.

"She bought one for everyone in the family. Was convinced the author was onto something. But that's Aunt Cya for you. Don't even get me started about our family trip to Washington D.C. after she watched the National Treasure movies."

Hector scooted to the edge of the couch cushion. "What's it about?"

"I don't know something about a portal to a parallel world. Didn't get past the first chapter. Way too slow."

Zoe set the book down in between them. Charity spotted a Grecian column on the front before Hector snatched it up to read the back.

Unfolding her pretzel legs, she leaned over to scan the blurb.

For Ever and Ever, Omen

Groan. And to make things worse, the author's picture on the back, of her in a steampunk dress and top hat, screamed, "I like to make terrible puns."

Huh, strange. That author did look familiar.

Ah yes, I retrieved fliers for her on that windy day, a while back.

> Jason Argo is just your average history-club
> obsessed eighth-grader. Until he discovers a
> portal to a parallel world in a local lake.

Hold up, a lake?

Just like the one she and Io had dipped into. This couldn't be a coincidence, right?

> One tubing accident gone wrong leads him
> into the world of Asphodel. In it, Asphodelians
> operate like zombies, quite unaware of their
> surroundings and enduring pitiful existences.
> He discovers that the Asphodelian curse
> spreads by physical touch, and that the curse is
> finding a way into his hometown, turning all
> his friends and families into the living dead.
> Will he find a way to stop the disease in time,
> and close the portal to Asphodel? Or will he get
> touched by the curse?

The author *had* to know about what happened to Io.

This is too crazy a coincidence not to be the same curse.

A pit dug into Charity's stomach. She laughed nervously. "Crazy ideas your aunt had, huh?"

"Yeah, well, we all need our hobbies, I guess." Zoe

popped a pearl into her mouth and collected her teacup and plate. She headed toward the kitchen. "You two have any other questions I can answer?"

Plenty, but something about the edge in her voice made Charity think it wasn't really a question, merely a kind gesture.

Plus she didn't want to blow the situation. After all, for once, because of how Charity helped direct the conversation, they actually got answers. Maybe she was starting to lose the stupids.

She glanced at a clock with ballet dancers in place of the hands. They were nearly at four o clock. And with the winters here, it would get dark within the hour. "We really should get going, but thanks for the tea."

As Charity went to collect her cup, she bumped her knee against the spine of the book.

"Umm, Zoe?"

"Yes?"

"Mind if we borrow this?"

Zoe perched a hand on her hip in the kitchen and squinted at Charity. Something told her this woman forgot to put in contacts today. Then Zoe threw her arms up.

"Please, take it off my hands. One less reminder."

Charity held back a grin, and then remembered she was no longer playing Delphonian Hoplites, and lets her lips split her cheeks. She hugged the book and made an X across her chest with her arms.

Right as she rose from the cushion, a doorbell rang. Its

ring echoed off the purple-painted walls.

Zoe's hands went right back to their station on her hips. "Bout time the food delivery people arrived. Have dance practice in an hour."

She glided toward the front door, whilst Charity tried to walk down the hallway and read the book at the same time. Moments later, she smacked into the wall.

Who knew literature could be so deadly.

"Umm, you look a little young to be delivering wings." Zoe's voice all but evaporated at the front door. The winter air must've stolen it.

Charity's toes scrunched the shaggy carpet on the way to the front door to retrieve her sandals. She watched her feet to make sure they didn't trip over one another.

"Sorry, miss, there's no easy way to ask this, but we were wondering if you could tell us about your cousin, Helen."

Her ears pricked at the familiar voice. She lifted her neck—at the expense of her clown feet—and caught the eyes of the kids stationed on the front stoop.

Danae and Paris.

Chapter 31

Should've Suspected Danae Might Have a Doppelganger. . . .

orry, kids, but I'm all out of bubble tea. Better luck next time."

All of them now on the front porch received a cheery door slam to the face. Pink, feeble clouds failed to cover a deep, blue sky above. An hour or so until sunset. Charity tucked her arms into her toga and turned to Danae.

"Is thirteen a little early to begin working for a wing franchise?" Charity smirked.

Danae rolled her eyes and jerked her chin at a gray minivan stationed at the bottom of the driveway. "Maybe we should take this conversation somewhere warmer."

All agreed, they hunched against the gale that tore at their cheeks.

"You were right," Danae grumbled, "about trying to uncover Cassandra's past. Paris told me that since we're all cursed that kind actions don't seem to affect us the same way. Even if it does, it seems worth the risk to try and save I—"

Sharp wind cut off her final words. Even in the blistering cold, nothing but warmth filled Charity's stomach.

They're trying to help Io, too.

Remnants of the Big Sad ebbed away in her shoulders. She didn't have to do this alone.

Does this mean we're finally an actual coalition?

They reached the van and climbed into the middle and back rows. Up front, a woman with gray strands interweaving a raven braid texted on a phone. Danae's mom, Charity assumed, or a doppelgänger of her from the future. Never wanted to assume too much too early.

"We've been following your trail from a distance," Danae said. "Paris has been filling me in with what clues you've found so far, and we're doing what we can to piece the rest of the puzzle."

So she *had* seen Danae at the ugly Christmas tree show.

Hector, scrunched in the back seat, eyed the driver warily. He leaned toward Danae who had chosen a middle seat adjacent to him.

"Maybe we should hold off this conversation, otherwise your driver might get weirded out by this curse stuff?"

Said literally the only other non-Coalition member in the car aside from Danae's mom slash time travel doppelgänger.

Danae belted her arms after she plugged in her seatbelt buckle. "It's fine, watch." With gloves, she tapped her mother's coated shoulder. "Hey, Mom, mind taking us to Lake

Prespa by the school? We're going to bring back some missing friends and stop a curse."

"Mmm, what? Sure sweetheart." Although her mother's skin yielded no gray tint, her voice matched those of Charity and Stefan's moms.

With a simper, Danae whipped back to Hector. "Sometimes you don't need a curse to be apathetic."

Her mom up front continued to tap away at her phone as she yanked the gear into drive and sped off.

"Anyway," Danae blinked several times, "Charity, do me a favor and dig out the thirteen-sided die in your pocket."

Charity's eyes bulged.

How did she know—?

"Paris mentioned the die," Danae nudged Paris, who decided it was a good time for a pre-curse-busting nap in the middle seat, "and Stefan talked after you and Hector left for Zoe's house. Now, die me."

Ideas about Danae's possible telepathic abilities bouncing in her skull, Charity dug out the gray die and placed it in Danae's palm. The other cupped the triskaidecagon and squinted at it in the pale pink light from the sun that spilled through the windows.

"Just as I thought. I planted this at the park when I saw the note on the Pawn Shoppe table a few weeks back. Went to check it out on Friday, but the die had gone missing."

Io had found the die.

"But this thing was red before I put it at the park. Means the curse is spreading."

Hector frowned and rubbed some whiskers on his chin. "Wait a moment. I lost one of my crimson die a few weeks back."

Danae smirked at Paris. And Paris either snickered or snored, hard to tell with the heat blasting overhead.

Charity daubed some sweat off her lips with her techie gloves and scanned the different textured fabric for the fingers. "So, the curse turns things gray?"

"Physically and metaphorically, it seems. Makes people apathetic, weary, like zombies. Like it sucks all the joy, all the purpose, all the kindness from people. And it also seems to have an effect on technology. Io'd told me about the heater in the car."

"But Stefan said his Mom turned gray, and she hasn't been to that park in years," Paris pointed out.

OK, so definitely a snicker and not a snore.

"Everyone in the Coalition is like a moving park, I guess." Danae shrugged. "Everything we touch turns to gray. And I don't know how long we're immune to the effects."

Zoe's book dug a corner into Charity's leg when they hit a pothole.

"Io also didn't go missing at the park," Charity pressed the book against her leg to hold it steady, "she disappeared at the lake." She reached around the middle seat and slid the book into Danae's lap. "Zoe's aunt, Cya, was obsessed with this book. And right before Cassandra disappeared, she had a run-in with Cya. Can't be a coincidence. And if it is, at least we got some bubble tea out of it."

Danae scanned the back cover for a minute. Her mother's texting keyboard taps filled the silence in the car.

"So," Danae filtered pages through her fingertips, like a fan, "you think the lake is where the portal to the curse is?"

Charity explained about the seaweed sensation that wrapped around her ankle during initiation. She winced in anticipation for comments like, "That's a stupid idea, Charity. Kidnapping monsters in lakes? No wonder people don't think you should be in normal people classes." Paris, now wide awake, mirrored Danae's mom and tapped away at his phone.

"And that's where you think Io went? To Asphodel?" Danae asked.

Paris shot up a hand. "Not Asphodel. Delphos."

Bright white light stung their eyes from a moment.

Goodness, how high does this kid kick up the brightness setting on his tablet?

Lo, once the blindness dissipated, she saw the Wikipedia listing for the game Delphonian Hoplites.

"Stefan and I were talking about video games, and I was trying to find out why Hector was so obsessed with this game," Paris said. "We did some digging and, check out who invented it."

Created by: Cya Tiresias

Chapter 32

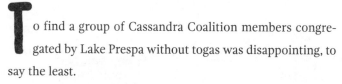

Would've Packed the Clown Shoes if There Was More Time. . . .

To find a group of Cassandra Coalition members congregated by Lake Prespa without togas was disappointing, to say the least.

Charity tripped on gravel rocks as she skittered toward them. The group un-broke from their blobbish circle and welcomed her with thin-lined lips and furrowed brows. Poker faces, on the house.

"Here's what we know," Danae barked this behind her and held up Zoe's book. She'd skimmed fifty pages on the drive over to the lake, while Charity counted the number of potholes they hit, "there's likely a portal to a parallel world in that lake."

She flicked her arm toward the water and almost flung the book at the surface.

"Inside it, we will find humanoid beings who operate very similar to Delphonian Hoplite players. Drained of their life force, apathetic, and from what I can tell about chapter five of this book—if the author would stop using so many fancy words—is that they can transfer the curse by touch."

Danae flicked the pages through her fingertips. Harsh wind bit their cheeks.

"Delphos is a lot like Ancient Greece, with limited technology and zombie-like people. That could explain why the curse affects tech and electricity. Now, we'll need to blend in with the people there. I think we should only take a small group of people, in case something goes wrong. Plus, we need to warn people if that curse is planning on breaking through the portal."

Shoulders slumped. Legs bobbled back and forth. Charity, on the other hand, bubbled with so much bubble tea, she thought the pearls would spit right out of her stomach like a cannon.

I hope I get to be on the actual rescue mission to save Io.

At last, Paris, who was knuckling his eyes from a nap interrupted, spoke. "You really think people are going to believe us? It sounds crazy. And no one believed *the* Cassandra. The Ancient Greek Cassandra, anyway, whenever she told people about bad things to come."

Danae wedged the toe of her black boot into the hard sand that lined the brittle, brown grass. Ice had melted from the lake's edges, and left behind dark, smoky waters.

"True, but we have to try. It's the right thing to do, and," she blew out a breath, "the nice thing, too. Now, who are we going to send?"

The group appeared to take a brave and courageous collective step back away from the lake. Wiry trees let the wind whistle through their branches. Everyone found their shoes incredibly fascinating for the next few seconds.

Anger bubbled in Charity's stomach. Well, if you wanted a job done right . . . . "I'm going."

In clear and full approval, Danae pinched her nose. "No, Charity. That would be a terrible idea. Can you go even two seconds without showing some sort of emotion?"

Tears pricked Charity's eyes. "Please, you have to let me. She's my best friend."

Exhale from Danae. "I know you have a beautiful heart, but altruism is a weakness, especially in Delphos. They'll be able to sniff you out a mile away."

Danae motioned to Hector. "You seem to be our resident Hoplite expert, wanna tag along?"

With a bow, twirl of the wrist, and a "m'lady" Hector appeared to accept her offer.

"That really should be enough, one for each person we need to bring back."

A stinging sensation filled Charity's forehead. She'd grown used to the feeling of rejection from her other peers. She rubbed the skin and tried to make the itchiness go away.

It's probably for the best. You want Io rescued. So if that happens, maybe that means keeping yourself away.

"Paris." Danae flicked her braid at him. "Did you bring the gray sheets so we can wear gray togas and blend in?"

Paris motioned for two Coalition members to part and rolled out a yellow suitcase with a Mickey Mouse design. He kicked the bag down and kneeled in a muddy patch of grass to unzip the main pocket. He unfurled two wrinkled sheets that, Charity assumed, had hung in Hector's basement. Danae and Hector tried to form the garments around their outfits to form some semblance of a toga. The former succeeded, the latter, 6/10, more of a tunic.

Let's hope the Delphonians didn't have too many history classes.

"Now," Danae clapped her hands together and scowled. She inspected the palms. "Shoot. I think there are holes in my gloves. I know we really can't pass the curse onto Cassandra or Io, but can't be too careful. And we wanna cover up in case the Delphonians wanna hold hands."

She scanned the crowd and her roan eyes landed on Charity.

"Mind letting me borrow your gloves?"

Well, they were Hector's to begin with. He'd never asked for the techie gloves back.

Besides, it's for the best you're not going. You'll ruin everything, like always, and this is something you cannot ruin.

Danae unsheathed her gloves and discarded them near some frail bull rushes. Frost bent the necks of the plants.

Chest tight and a million pounds heavier, Charity peeled off the gloves from her hands and winced at the cold. Already the weather had turned her fingers pink.

Eyes sweating a great deal, she presented the gloves to Danae.

"Great, thanks for the hand protection. Now besides

Zoe, who doesn't really believe in the book's contents, we're the only ones who really know about the curse. Aside from the author, I suppose."

"And Cya," Hector offered.

Who decided to stake out some nice beach on Florida, according to Zoe.

"It's really important that you get the word out to as many people as possible." Danae breathed into her frozen, gloved hands. "Get people to layer up, so the Delphonians can't make physical contact. Coalition members seem to be the only ones immune to turning gray, so let's keep the contagion to a minimum."

Purple ink bled into the sky. They'd reach sunset soon. Without Hector, how would she get a ride home?

Maybe she could hitch one with all the Coalition members. Sure enough, in the parking lot up the winding path, cars puffed exhaust smoke from their tailpipes.

And then, her heartbeat skipped, she watched a figure clad in a toga trip up the path. He face-planted. Bounced up. And continued running.

Stefan's lolling tongue came into view as he puffed and hunched over. On his back, Bowser spikes jutted toward the sky.

Did he . . . steal her backpack? And then, like any good ol' thief, he decided to flaunt the goods in front of her? Well, she always knew he was jealous of that book bag. From the first day when she wore it at school, he said, "Why? Just . . . why?"

Clearly envy.

"S-sorry I'm l-late." He straightened and placed his hands on his waist to let in more air. "Had to have my m-mom drop me off at y-your house to pick up some things."

Whomp. He slipped the backpack off his shoulders, near the shoreline, and squatted to unzip the main pouch. Sand rustled around him as he placed various items from inside the bag onto the banks.

"Stefan?" Her voice crackled like a campfire in her throat.

He pulled out a propeller hat. The breeze caused the turbine to spin.

"Stefan."

A hand-me-down Furbie stuffed animal, a weird owl-shaped thing with a plume of hair on its crown from her cousin Verity, perched on the hat like a bird's nest.

"What is all of this?"

"Helping my best friend pack for her journey, of course."

Embers warmed Charity's heart and the stinging sensation from the rejection disappeared from her forehead.

Stefan thinks that I'm *the one who should rescue my best friend.*

Oxygen filled her chest until she felt she could float away like a helium balloon.

Creamed corn can in his fingertips, he paused, and rolled up his pant legs until they disappeared into his toga.

Must've felt the cold mud seep into his fabric too.

"We don't know how long she'll be there, and never

hurts to come prepared for any situation."

Danae slouched and drew her lips into a thin line. That was a good sign.

"We're full on passengers for Delphos." Danae huffed while Stefan placed Groucho glasses next to the Furbie. "Seriously, where'd you get that stuff? A prank store?"

"Charity's dresser. Would've grabbed more items, but we were running short on time, and it was a miracle I got my mom to get out of bed and to drive me to two places. She's getting grayer by the day."

Out popped a Ninja Turtles mask.

"Although, she does seem some days like she's really trying to fight it. I tried to bake a cake using a mix the other day, and that really perked her up. Especially after the whole 'my Uncle can't staunch the bleeding in his arm because of the rotisserie chicken' incident."

A pair of green dinosaur foot slippers rolled onto the sand.

"Maybe you should try doing that before you go to Delphos, Chair. The cake thing. Not the biting arm thing. That might perk your mom up. Ooh!"

He pulled out a tube of cinnamon roll mix. How long had she been keeping that on her dresser?

Danae snorted. "The Delphonians aren't going to stop unleashing a thirteen-year curse simply because someone baked them a cake."

Clearly, Danae had never had an ice cream cake from The Scoop.

"Stefan, stop. I already told Charity she isn't going to Delphos."

The hand-warming packet sensation left Charity's chest as Danae marched toward Stefan.

Stefan did not stop. He was busy digging out something stuffed at the bottom of the back.

"I said STOP!"

He flinched and threw Charity's squid-shaped stuffed animal over his shoulder. Inkheart landed in the lake and bobbled on a dark ripple. By now, the rim of the sky had turned almost black.

"Don't worry, Chair, I got it." Stefan crouched over the waters and gripped one of the tentacles of the stuffed animal. "Barely even wet. See, if we dry him off with one of those gray sheets back—whoa!"

Something inky, much like Inkheart's tentacles but black instead of bright green, wrapped around Stefan's arm. It must've yanked him, because a moment later, his upper half submerged into the lake.

Charity shot to her feet and bolted to the shore. She gripped his ankle with both hands and dug her sandals into the sand. Someone else roped their arms around her waist and pulled. Like a game of tug o' war, except way better, they inched their way backward. The back of Stefan's scalp surfaced, then his hand. And the black tendril unwound itself from Stefan's arm.

Moments later, when the tentacle released, Charity collapsed back. A quick glance over her shoulder, and five other bodies that had fallen into a domino line, indicated how many people had pulled him out of the lake.

The person right behind her, who broke her fall, Danae, had paled. "Charity. You weren't wearing gloves."

Blood left her cheeks, and she turned back to Stefan. His skin was sporting a blue color from the frozen lake temperatures.

Wait a moment, not blue . . . gray.

How did the curse react that fast? Danae was right . . . it had picked up the pace.

There was something beautiful about a zombified friend. How he hunched his back, eyes-half open in a stupor. Drool dribbling out of the side of his mouth might've been overkill, but leave it to living dead Stefan to overact.

She released his ankle, like it had burned her fingertips, and bolted to the side and upright. Danae somersaulted to the right, perhaps to get Paris's arms off her waist, and flicked sand off her nose.

"It's fine, everyone. Remember, as Coalition members, we're immune to t—"

Stefan lurched forward and gripped Paris's forearm. Blots of gray spread throughout Paris's skin, like milky bubble tea.

First thought: Oh, cool!

Second thought: Oh no.

The curse could transfer to everyone, even the Coalition peeps now. Charity bunched up her fingers in the loose fabric on her toga and raced over to Danae. With a layer of fabric in between the skin, she grabbed Danae's wrist and helped her to her feet.

"No time. We need to get to Delphos," Charity said. She whipped her head over her shoulder and watched the rest of the Coalition scatter, chased by three already-zombified members. One hunched over Coalition member chased Hector into the woods. So much for him going on the rescue mission.

Not taking no for an answer, or at least, ignoring the "No, no, no, no," Danae shrieked, Charity raced with her in tow into the water and waited.

Come on, little squid lake monster. We have some nice juicy ankles for you.

Freezing water stung her skin, and sand squished underneath her sandals. Where had their tentacled friend gone?

Paris, still at the shore's edge, turned and lumbered toward them. They backed down a bank, until the sand dropped off, and left them bobbling. Zombies appeared not to be allergic to water, and Paris sloshed into the lake, foam bubbles popping around him.

Here, squiddy, squiddy, squiddy. Here, boy. Or girl. Or whatever, just eat us.

Five feet separated them and Paris. Something about the thick folds of the togas made swimming an impossible task. The sheets kept catching on their arms.

Something tight and slimy burned her cold ankles as it wound its way up to her calves.

About time.

Chapter 33

Should've Brought Some Watercolor Paint....

Review of drowning: two stars, takes way too long.

Charity waited at the bottom of the lake, while the slimy decaying plant matter and sand chewed on her ankles. Like quicksand that wanted to take its sweet ol' time.

Mouth bubbling, she glanced upward at the dark surface. Hazy bits of colorful light drifted downward. They'd reach night any minute now.

Speaking of now, the sluggish sand had reached her knees and slopped over her sweats. She squeezed her eyes shut and hoped she could pass out or fall asleep in the time it took the lake to eat her. One Mississippi, two Mississippi . . . .

The high-pitched "eee" disappeared from her eardrums, and the cold sensation from the frigid waters had disappeared too. Instead, now dry, she flung open her eyes and slumped onto a patch of gray dirt.

"What the—?" Danae sagged right next to her and stared ahead into a misty gray fog.

Charity glanced at her surroundings. They were in a field of white flowers with six petals. Asphodelian flowers, if she remembered right from pictures Stefan had shown her when he got obsessed with Greek mythology and the underworld.

Next to the field was a hill that led up to buildings. They were pillared, much like all the photos she'd seen of Greek ruins. Except, this time, they looked black and white. Everything here did.

It also felt like everything from the Big Sad had come back. Her movements were sluggish. She waved her arm back and forth and felt as if someone had thrust it into Jell-O. Heaviness pulled her to the ground, and everything was silent.

Much like how Charity wanted to be on bad days with the Big Sad. Alone, in her room, in darkness, in silence.

Oh, how she did not miss this. How this place looked and felt like the exact opposite of Almsgiving.

In the dim lighting, Danae's skin, braid, everything looked as though someone had transported her into a black and white photo.

Danae patted the ground and swallowed, blinking. "Where did the lake go?"

Twisted trees, the haunted kind, had sprouted up in random places in between the Grecian columns. The fog that surrounded the flowers had started to wither into a weak mist.

"Maybe we're in the lake's stomach," Charity suggested.

"We're not in anyone's stomach," Danae snapped, and then pinched her nose. "Delphos must not want us to exit the way we came in."

Fire flickered in Danae's eyes. Or at least, in the gray lighting, it was a bright white spark. She rose. Charity followed, surprised how the fabric on her toga didn't cling to her skin like it had moments before.

"Why don't we get our bearings?" Danae patted her sides, where pockets would go, and groaned. "Great, left the book behind. Now, how are we going to navigate this place?"

"Speaking of, where is this place? Is it at the bottom of the lake?"

Danae frowned. "From what I could tell in the first fifty pages of that book, Delphos used to be a town like Almsgiving before the curse spread. Like Atlantis, after it got cursed, it sunk to where no one could find it—at least, that was the general gist I was getting from it. The author had some whacko ideas."

Mist slithered around their ankles like snakes. Whoever had fog machine duty in Delphos left for too long a snack break. Charity squinted at the vapor.

A sudden energy flooded her veins. They'd arrived.

Time to find Io.

Although Charity had never mastered being able to tell distances of things, a town was well within sight, perched on a hill. Maybe a half-mile away, she guessed. It looked like a similar distance to her co-op's half-mile run back in elementary school.

Not one, but multiple Grecian columns lined what looked like the downtown shops. Hunched figures formed silhouettes in sheaths of light, coming from above, like spotlights on a lake's surface.

"Maybe we can ask the nice creepy shadows for directions."

Elbows swinging, Charity set off toward the agora, only seconds later finding a band of cloth-covered arms wrapped around hers that tugged backward. The lake monster impersonation, played by Danae.

"Do you remember anything that we talked about at the lake?" Danae hissed. "If we go up to any Delphonian bright-eyed and bushy-tailed, they're going to sense we don't belong here."

Charity's face flamed. "Well, what should we do?"

"We gotta blend in. Act sluggish, apathetic."

The sluggish part wouldn't be a problem. Something felt off about the gravity here. Like they'd attached barbells to Charity's calves and arms. Memories from the park reeled. Hadn't the mulch tugged her downward there, too, like a magnetic pull? Danae's voice yanked her out of Semele.

"Luckily, everything here's grayscale, so we don't need to worry about looking the part. Even your white toga can pass for silver. Now, for acting like we belong in Delphos . . . ."

Charity's neck hunched. "I'm not really that good at blending in. I get if you'd want to split ways and find Io on your own." The itchiness from Danae's previous rejection stung her forehead again.

Danae frowned and then shook her head, braid whipping over her shoulder. "And lose someone else to Delphos? No, we'll just have to find ways to help you fake it."

She stepped behind Charity and pushed her shoulders down, touching only fabric, until a U formed on Charity's spine.

"You know, for heavy gravity affecting us, your back sure isn't acting like it."

When she released, Charity's spine uncurled a little.

"OK, forget the back—"

Danae squared her fabric-clad shoulders until they faced each other like a mirror.

"—let's focus on facial expressions. Give me a blank look. No smile, vacant eyes. Let's see your best shot."

Charity's lips twitched as she attempted to wriggle them downward in a Scrooge fashion. As for the vacant eyes . . . she flung open her eyelids as wide as they could go.

"Nope, now you just look like a serial killer."

It was so hard to tell whether Danae had complimented or insulted her. With a groan through gritted teeth, Danae paced off to the side. White flowers crunched underneath her sandals. She paused, and she brightened. Charity scanned the soupy skies for some form of sunlight, but besides the random pokes of spotlight, no main source of heat showed itself.

Rip.

No, no one died. Danae tore a piece of her sheet off, around her ankles, and she waved the split cloth like a flag. She then draped the fabric over Charity's head like a hood and tucked the loose strands into Charity's toga. The new veil obscured her peripherals and shielded all but her pointy nose.

"Keep your head toward the ground and don't make eye

contact with anyone. Hopefully, people won't look too closely at your face. Now, let's explore."

Charity stooped her neck and followed Danae's sandals up a prickly grassy hill and toward the 'downtown' shops. Strange and faint smells caught her pointy nose when they reached the entrance to the town. She glanced upward. The veil covered half her face, but she managed to spy a large square archway with the words "Δέλφος" engraved on the center.

"Wonder what that means," Danae muttered.

Eyes back on the sandals, she got a close look at the Delphonian footwear of people around her. Shoes with braided straps wound around toes and ankles appeared to be in vogue. She prayed she'd never have to see a Delphos runway show and scanned the rest of the marble slabs of stone for something interesting.

Nearby stubby gray feet, a basket full of either dates or cockroaches, so hard to tell in black and white, rested next to a wooden sign that stated, in sloppy black paint, "Δρχ"

Stefan sometimes liked to draw Greek words in his notes for class. She thought that one stood for drachma. They must pay for things in Ancient Greek currency here.

If this place was Ancient Greece, or like it, they must've had the same hierarchy mentioned in her Ancient history class. Their teacher, during that unit, had divided them into different social strata.

Sure enough, a beggar in rags sat with a hand held out nearby a stall. No one gave her any coins. Right next to her, a man with a tired sort of face covered some vases with black paint swirls.

She kept looking up. She couldn't help it. Everyone looked human, more or less, with a little drool glistening on their lips.

Was Danae right? Had this town once been a place like Almsgiving, and everyone here ended up cursed somehow? If so, would that make the Delphonians just like humans only with a problem swallowing their saliva?

Danae shot her a dirty look. Charity re-hunched her head.

Toga edges swayed and revealed ankles and more sandals. Charity wondered if the costume change came after one got cursed.

How would that work? Did they have zombie seamstresses who inspected the new arrivals with gray tape measures?

ZOMBIE SEAMSTRESS: And for the waist, you're measuring at a 38.

NEW ZOMBIFIED ARRIVAL: I'm a 36!

ZOMBIE SEAMSTRESS: They're togas. They're shapeless outfits anyway. This whole tape measuring business is just so I can keep a job in this meaningless, bureaucratic economy. You'll get a bedsheet like everyone else.

NEW ZOMBIFIED ARRIVAL: I like to think of us as an oligarchic democracy.

ZOMBIE SEAMSTRESS: Quiet, you!

Danae's feet had disappeared from the dusty path in front of her. She snapped her neck up and found the raven braided girl next to a wooden stake. Four stakes held up a striped covering. Underneath, a Delphonian man displayed various cheeses. One stunk of peppers.

Huh. That reminded her of the Big Sad. Sometimes only the strongest foods had taste. Everything else had the flavor of dust, except for spicy salsas and her mom's attempts to make Indian curry in the kitchen.

She huddled next to one pole and got a better look at the zombies milling the marketplace. Sure enough, like Stefan, they supported a neck hunch and lumbered forward. But nothing distinguished them much from humans. No arm growing out of their forehead or anything else that could happen if one uncovered a mummy from an Egyptian pyramid and invoked a pox upon themselves.

Next to her, Danae feigned a dull interest in a white cheese blob in a pottery bowl.

"Why do you think they have a marketplace in the first place?" Charity whispered and wriggled her nose when flies buzzed around the dairy specimen. "They're zombies."

Or were they? She couldn't shake the wriggling feeling that they were, in fact, cursed humans.

"They're Delphonians," Danae corrected her, "and because spreading a curse takes cash and a booming economy I guess. Plus, where else are you going to get cheese?"

Anarchy and zombie apocalypses did have their setbacks.

"Now, hush, I want to try and listen in on some conversations to get clues as to what to do next."

Noise. That hadn't occurred to her at first. Even though they were dead in the center of downtown Delphos, most of the bustle came from the clink of coins or sizzle from a fire pit nearby. Did the people in this black and white world even talk?

A figure in a hood shuffled underneath the tent. Danae tucked her arms into her toga, to avoid the nearing touch, and the two girls shuffled to the side. The merchant behind the table, a Delphonian with a goatee, sifted drachma into a small, cinched bag.

Note to self: when you become a zombie, make sure to bring some zombie cows and get to acidifying that milk.

Cheese was clearly an untapped market in the undead world.

The Delphonian next to them unrolled the hood, tapped the table with her finger, and motioned for the merchant to slice her a chunk of crumbly white cheese. Charity's jaw sank when she spotted the static electricity hair.

"Io?"

Io's eyes widened, serial killer style, and she stared Charity down across the makeshift tent. Although difficult to tell a friend from a zombie in this lighting, Charity fought the nagging feeling that the drool that glistened on the corners of Io's lips didn't have to do with the cheese.

Charity tore off the veil on her head and wrapped it around her hand. Then, she gripped Danae's fingers and dragged her out of the tent's shade. Not that the glow from the lack of sun helped with either brightening the setting or

205

giving more heat.

"What are you—?" Danae let her fingers go slack while Charity continued to drag.

"Gotta go. She following us?"

Danae must've glanced over her shoulder because her yelp a second later confirmed the answer.

"Ooh, mama, yes, I've always wanted a chase scene." Charity broke into a sprint.

Chickens scattered in their pathway, and she dodged a woman who had a vase hoisted on her back.

Another note to self: use the zombie hunch to carry items.

Oh boy, she hoped she could remember all these tips once they passed the curse onto her.

Delphonians in the distance appeared to catch on to the excitement and formed a barricade twenty feet ahead. A horror and surprise, considering everyone moved sluggishly here. Arm in arm, and spanning from the makeshift tents to the marble-roofed shops, they looked like a group of zombie boss babes about to take over the world.

Yikes, how would they break through that crowd with all the exposed arms and legs? Even if she managed to slip underneath or past them, one would reach out and tag, "You're it." She halted.

Behind her, Io had gained. Danae must've turned over a basket full of fish because their zombified friend was busy circumventing scattered bass.

Something looped around her toga-clad arm and tugged her into a marble shop. Mummified hands shoved her and

Danae into a large basket, similar to the one housing the fish back on the street. The blurry figure slammed a lid on top of them. Gosh darn, she needed to invest in glasses soon.

Charity tucked herself as much as she could to avoid skin contact with Danae. She slowed her breathing and listened to the galumph of footsteps in the shop.

Light poked through holes in the basket's braids, not much else. Stomps rushed past them and disappeared into the distance moments later.

At last, she and her friend let out a breath.

The lid popped off, and Danae shimmied out first. "Where'd they go?"

A low female voice answered. "Delphonians aren't that hard to trick. Told them some *Zoans* rushed through my shop and out the back. Looked excited. Well, as excited as Delphonians go. We don't really see Zoans here."

Charity popped her head up, like a weasel, and observed their savior. A young woman, about Zoe's age, with hip-length curly dark hair, a large nose, and shiny bands up and down her arms. Even though the bracelets were gray, Charity would've liked to think they were gold in another parallel world.

This woman would've belonged to a higher class. At least, not beggar asking for drachma status.

No doubt, her eyes had a spark of life, and praise! No drool on her lips.

Danae smoothed out some wrinkles in her own toga. "Anyway, thanks for saving us—"

"Cassandra." She smirked. "Don't mention it."

Chapter 34

Should've Consulted My Editor First (Sorry, Editor). . . .

Wow.

The Cassandra. OG curse woman. The lady, the myth, the non-zombie.

. . . I thought she'd be taller.

Cassandra smoothed down her toga and pushed herself onto a marble countertop. She shoved aside some mini stacked amphorae. Corks stoppered what Charity could guess was some liquid inside, like olive oil or hydrofluoric acid. Whatever goes on the breadsticks at restaurants.

Then Cassandra clapped her palms on her knees.

"I'll give you three ques-tions. Total. We don't have much time, and Delphonians can sense curiosity a mile away."

While Charity climbed out of the basket and marveled at how her friend managed to do this without tripping on her toga (oh right, she had torn it at the bottom), Danae flung out an arm.

"I got this, Chair. We're cursed but we're not zombies, our friend Io is both cursed and now part of the legions of the undead. Explain."

A sing-song laugh bobbled in Cassandra's throat. "That wasn't a question, more like an imperative statement, but I suppose we'll have to make do."

At last, Charity had eased herself out of the basket. She steadied her balance on the rim and pulled out the rest of her toga.

"Let's start with the curse. As you may have guessed, any human who is particularly known for their kindness has gotten it. Anything we touch turns to, well . . . ." She pinched a drachma coin purse to her left. "The opposite of gold. That's actually what did happen to the Delphonians here. The curse had spread throughout their town. Then the town vanished. I'm not sure how many years ago. Maybe hundreds. They don't seem to remember."

So the Delphonians were humans, not just undead.

Cassandra set down the bag.

"Anyway, back to the curse. It's an omen of sorts, to hint at what's to hit your world. Bad luck. Heard plenty of Delphonians talk about it. They've been waiting for this event for some time. I guess curses is as curses does. Once you get bit by the bug, you gotta spread it."

Charity steadied herself again so she wouldn't tumble headfirst into the basket. The gravity here didn't help with the dizziness that had taken over her skull.

Food fights, her grandma's cranberry sauce, everything happened as a warning. She was the omen.

They all were.

"Since I got here, I've only seen Delphonians until your Zoan friend arrived not too long ago. Until she got initiated."

Zoan must've meant from Earth. Or at least, from a city on Earth not cursed yet.

Danae flicked up an eyebrow. A fly swirled around her head.

"Initiated."

"Oh dear, with the way your voice went up, that did sound like a question, but we won't count it. Yes. She got contaminated by the Delphonian touch. Seems they transferred the ability to curse people—to turn them into Delphonians—to us, as, when she came into my shop—" She stared at her palms. "Well, let's say bad luck seems to follow me."

Teeth crashed onto Charity's tongue to hold back the obvious question: Were you the one who transformed Io?

She let out a breath and stared at a large amphora with swirl designs etched onto the pottery.

OK, Chair, what do you know so far?

1. The Coalition's members got cursed with an omen. Anything kind they did backfired. Like bad luck.

2. The Coalition members and Delphonians could transfer the Delphonian sickness via physical touch. But the Coalition people could also get infected if they got touched. A double whammy.

3. Put a couple nice, gray planters in this shop and some jazz music, and this place would be the bee's knees in the summer.

"Question one: answered. Next?"

Danae rested an index finger under her chin. Pause. She brightened as much as one could do in grayscale.

"You said the Delphonians are going to hit our world. What do you mean by that?"

"Finally, an actual question." Cassandra clapped her palms and rubbed. "Thirteen years ago, two portals opened, one inside Delphos, and one out. The four of us took the portal at the lake."

She jumped off the countertop and glided toward shelves that lined the wall, full of mini vases. "Delphos is getting too crowded. They need to expand. That's why they don't let too many people into the lake route. The problem is, when their city vanished from earth and showed up here there was nowhere else to go, except for right here in this city. What they don't realize is, if they curse a whole human earth town, it'll probably vanish again. And they'll go back to square zero."

That would explain how so many people went boating and fishing on Lake Prespa without consequences. Charity tried to imagine Almsgiving disappearing from existence altogether, like objects at the Bermuda Triangle or pies at Thanksgiving.

A vase nosedived off the shelf and Cassandra dove and caught it. Returned the vessel to its small area of space on the shelf.

"Of course, exceptions do happen. Krakkie's been getting hungry. Overcrowding means food shortages. So our little lake monster's been swallowing a few new visitors. Don't worry."

Her eye caught Charity's.

"You're still alive. Krakkie feeds off dead skin cells. It's like a pore strip, but slimier and makes weird squeaky noises that echo in the night when you're trying to sleep. Which, of course, you hear because everyone else in this town is dead silent."

Cassandra turned back to the shelves and grabbed two vases, one the size of a chipmunk and the other, a chunky raccoon.

"As for the nature of the portals," she placed both vases on the countertop and motioned for the girls to stand beside her, "the one in the lake opened wide thirteen years ago. Entire humans and lake monsters can fit in it. And really, the only reason, we can't exit via the lake is Krakkie done plugged herself into the hole, so now no one can get out that way."

Two fingers tapped the rim of the larger raccoon-sized vase. That represented Lake Prespa.

"The other portal," she rubbed a thumb on a snail-spiral handle on the 'chipmunk' vase, "is considerably smaller. It's widened over time, but it's taken thirteen years for it to get to the size of a Delphonian. Once it's large enough, the invasion will begin."

She gripped the necks of both vases and returned them to the shelf.

"To give you another freebie, since I can see the question on your lips, no. The Delphonians don't do 'live in peace with our neighbors.' Their touch automatically turns everything gray, so even if they did have a heart, they couldn't help but curse everything and everyone."

Images from the park flittered across her eyes. How the thirteen-sided die turned gray. But why didn't she transform into a Delphonian when she held it?

Maybe it required direct physical contact from a Delphonian themselves. Or, in Io's case, a girl laden with the Cassandra curse.

Either way, she wouldn't waste their last question on something like that.

Footsteps echoed behind her. She flinched and glanced over her shoulder as a large Delphonian woman surveyed a long-necked vase on a shelf at the front of the store. Charity forced her attention on the shelf nearest to herself. Remember, no curiosity. They could smell it.

With a grunt, the woman headed for the exit. Charity watched through shelves as she disappeared.

"Business has been down lately." Cassandra twirled the drawstring on the coin purse around her finger. "People think the vases are going to be grayer on the other side of the portal. It's hard to tell. People here don't display much emotion."

She paused and set her jaw.

"Sometimes, it's easier that way."

Gravity tugged on Charity's ribcage. She slumped to the stone floor and pretzeled her legs. Danae remained standing

213

but had leaned her hip against a column.

"We still have one question."

"That you do."

Danae formed a triangle with her leg when she leaned back. "There are just so many that I could ask. This whole situation's bizarre."

Charity traced dents in the stone floor with her fingers. She liked the way the grooves felt smooth and rough at the same time. Io had once taught her this trick to remember test answers.

"You just keep drawing circles until the definition or term pops into your head."

Oh, Io . . . she blinked away the images of her friend, now zombified. This was a lot to take in. When would she see that happy, smiling expression she'd grown used to all these years?

Circle, circle, circle.

Unless they found a way to reverse the curse to get Io un-Delphonian-ed.

Wait a moment . . . .

As she drew circles, a question popped into her head. *The* question.

Her chin lifted, and she watched Danae for any signs she'd hijack the final query. Her friend was still thinking. She lifted her arm and Cassandra sniggered into her fist.

"This isn't a classroom."

Pause.

"Yes?"

"What happened thirteen years ago?"

Lights died in Cassandra's eyes.

Had I asked the wrong one?

Or like, back at Zoe's house, she said the right words to get the truth they needed.

Cassandra's head hunched toward the floor, and she leaned back into the countertop to support her spine. Chickens revved their wings outside of the shop.

Cassandra's low voice drew her back. "In fairness, I did give you three questions." She licked her lips and sighed. "It might be easier to show than to tell you the story."

Chapter 34.5

Could've, Should've, Would've. . . .

Thirteen Years Ago

"Did someone glue that book to your nose?"

The girl peeked out from behind the cover that featured Grecian columns. Half the book shielded her face. But not enough to disguise the steel, gray eyes. She disappeared back behind the cover, and Cassandra made a note of the dandelions woven into the girl's dark hair.

No wonder she didn't attract anyone to her lunch table. Memories from their seventh-grade year flooded her mind. How the girl would always be stationed alone in the cafeteria. How Cassie had suggested their band table make room from one more seat, but no one scooted their chair to the side.

So she stayed with them and chewed on her peanut butter and banana sandwich.

Cassandra clawed at her arm, cheeks hot. When would they turn up the AC in this bookstore?

"Sorry to bother you, but the owner looks busy."

She jabbed a thumb over her shoulder. The owner, a man with a mustache that made walruses bow in shame during no-shave November, was busy waving customers over to an author perched at a table by the corner. How they managed to fit her, her hoop skirt dress and twenty books in one section of the store could confound any Holmes or Christie.

"Anyway, for my summer project, I got assigned oracles in Ancient Greece. Any clue where I can find a book like that?"

One finger poked out from the cover. "Downstairs."

"Thanks, I—-youch, where'd you get a bruise like that?"

With a heavy sigh, the girl slammed the book onto her lap and flaunted the purple-splotched finger. "I bruise easily. It's a blood condition."

"Right, that answers how it's possible that you can get it. But you never explained how you acquired that specific and fine specimen."

The girl shielded her fingers with her other palm. "Basketball camp at school. One of the girls *accidentally* jammed it." It seemed she would've made air quotes, but a purple finger made that a little impossible.

Heaviness clouded Cassie's chest for a moment. Then, she brightened.

"You know, nothing heals a hurt finger more than a dip in cool water. My family's heading out tonight to go boating at Lake Prespa. Wanna join?"

Light lit up the girl's cheeks. She straightened in her chair stationed between shelves. "Sounds fun." She halted, lips slack. "Why are you being nice to me? I don't even know your name."

"Cassie. And because it never hurts to be kind. Your name?"

"Helen."

"Helen," Cassie reached out her hand to shake and then retracted like the bruise had burned her own skin. "Nice to meet you, best friend."

*****

"You really need to tell your coach." Cassandra shoved her hands into her pockets. "That girl clearly bonked you on the back of the head with a basketball to give you a concussion."

Helen shivered and squinted at the bright light that poked through slate clouds. They turned to the right and up the path to Semele Park.

"I mean, I get they're annoyed because you're 'too nice to be a basketball player' and that's seen as 'weak' or something, but they took away your favorite hobby. Now you can't read because she gave you a head injury. We honestly shouldn't even be out here. You need to be resting."

They slumped onto a bench and watched the empty playground. With October fading into November, few kids had visited Semele. No doubt to avoid early frostbite by clinging to anything metallic here. Still, a shame, especially because the city had slapped everything with a fresh coat of colorful paint.

"Cass," Helen puffed out a dragon breath, "I appreciate the concern, but you know I needed to get out of the house. With Mom and all her conspiracy theories about that book."

She kicked a mulch chunk with her sneaker's toe.

"Besides, don't make me feel guilty on top of having this awful headache." She grimaced.

"Guilty?"

"For inviting me to the lake, sitting at my lunch table, talking with me by my locker, and now you're trying to take care of me when I have a concussion. My mom cried, you know, when I came home and told her I'd finally made a friend at school."

"Helen—"

"Well, well."

Cassandra shot to her feet and Helen followed, slower. They spun around and found a group of skyscraper girls in Northface jackets. The tallest, a girl with winged eyeliner, pursed her lips and nestled a basketball on her hips.

"Shouldn't you be in bed?"

Shaking, Helen paced back two steps. Cassandra barred her with an arm. She glanced over her shoulder and noticed a basketball court a sidewalk path away from the playground.

"Deaf, Helen?" The girl rolled the basketball in her palms like a crystal ball. "Don't tell me the concussion knocked out your hearing."

"You've done enough damage," Cassandra barked. "Now, why don't you head to those courts back there, and leave her alone?"

The girl perched a thin eyebrow. "Careful, Cass. Just because you don't bruise easily doesn't mean you can't get a matching concussion."

They locked eyes for two seconds. Then, Cassie dropped her arm.

"Good, now, Helen, I'm concerned you aren't taking your bedrest seriously. I'm thinking you're faking the concussion so you can get out of doing gym."

Their school had an exception to having to participate in gym class: participation in a full season of a sport.

"Now, I'll give you the count of three to run back to your mom's car before things get ugly. One."

"Cass," Helen mouthed the words. "Please."

Tingles ran up and down Cassie's neck. Tears stung her eyes because her legs wouldn't move from her spot. Like the mulch had bitten down on her feet.

"Two."

Unbalanced, and disoriented from the concussion, Helen turned on her heels. And headed straight for the monkey bars behind her.

At the same time the girl said "Three," she chucked the ball. Missed, but Helen rammed her forehead right into the monkey bars when she ducked from the throw.

*****

Probability of dying from a concussion: Not likely.

Probability of dying from a second concussion that happens right after the first one: Much higher.

Probability of dying from all the conditions above with a

bruising disorder: R.I.P.

And no, we're not talking about togas this time.

*****

"I was informed by one of the girls on Helen's team that you scared her and made her ram her head into the monkey bars."

"Ms. Tiresias, the girls on her team made her run away. They scattered after she got injured."

"Put that handbell down, dear. We're not done with the conversation. This little charity event you've arranged isn't going to help with the fact that my daughter is dead, and you were the only one at the playground when I got out of the car."

"It wasn't me!"

"Then what did you do when they supposedly taunted her? When they threw a ball at her, as you claim? Did you stand up to them? Try everything in your power to prevent them from hurting her?"

Silence.

"A pox on you."

More silence.

"And I just found the perfect curse to do the trick."

Deadly silence.

"For you, and anyone else whose façade hides the ugly monster underneath."

Chapter 35

Could've Gone on the Slip 'n Slide of Death. . . .

Danae scrunched her nostrils. "Why the heck would you illustrate that story on a bunch of vases?"

The three girls sat on the floor of Cassie's shop, surrounded by vases with depictions of Chapter Thirty-Three point five. Cassandra's lips twitched and she leaned forward to clasp the handle of one with a trumpet-shaped lid. In black, a squid monster pulled a girl down into a lake.

"I said I'd show it to you rather than tell you. And besides, after you spend months learning from the best Delphonian potter how to fire up that kiln three separate times, you put those art skills to good use. It's a good thing a really nice artisan family took me in. Not the highest of classes here, but they took care of me. Some Delphonians seem to be fighting against their curse. Gives me hope."

Just like Charity's mom at Thanksgiving. And Charity when she wrestled with the Big Sad. They all fought.

Her lip pulled like someone had tugged it with a fishing

hook.

"Granted, I probably shouldn't have sold some of those pieces of pottery." She gestured at some gaps in the floor where vases with supposed depictions of 'Cya invoking the thirteen-year curse that opened the portal' and 'Cassie's five hundredth attempt and failure to weave a shroud.' "But zombie cheese doesn't buy itself."

Charity pulled her knees up and rested her chin on them.

"I don't understand why Cya wouldn't believe you. Or why Helen couldn't just tell her, at the hospital, what really happened."

"Ah, I forgot I sold my 'Helen was in a coma until she died' vase. Delphonians really do like the painful ones, especially that weaving the shroud one. My artisan family was so disappointed in me—well, at least as disappointed as you can be as a zombie."

She flicked a curl shielding her nose. Her laugh had a crack on it, like her throat was made of the same materials as the marble floor.

"What I don't understand," Danae rubbed her thumb on a vase with a potter wagging a finger at a girl with long hair, "is how you managed to trick them for so long."

Charity hugged her arms. "How'd you go for years without physical contact? Without showing emotions?"

Cassandra pulled her legs in and tucked them underneath her thighs. In silence, she traced indiscernible patterns on the floor. She blew out a long breath.

"Community theater does do wonders."

No wonder she managed to snag the venue for her Christmas tree charity if she'd done performances for them.

"Besides," Cassandra rocked back and forth, "the atmosphere kind of brings you down. You learn to mimic it, initiated or not. And the people here don't care. As long as you don't make waves, you could just," she made jazz hands, "vanish."

Bones cracked as she rose to her feet.

"Now, as I have answered all three of your questions, we need to work on the most important part of your visit. Leaving."

She massaged her thigh. Perhaps from sitting too long.

"Our main objective is to get out of here, keep the Delphonians away from your world, and to close the portal. The curse is connected with it being open. The moment we get it shut, the connection should sever. Anyone initiated or cursed will get turned back to normal. At least," she shrugged, "that's what that book said."

Charity gawked at her shaking palms. Io, Stefan, her mom . . . all of them could turn back to their cheery selves. She could hug people again. Her arms warmed at the thought.

"We also need to get Io to the other side," Charity chimed in. "That is why we came here after all."

Danae frowned and sloshing echoed in the walls. Charity followed her glance and watched a marble water fountain with a pillar spigot spew water.

"Problem with that plan," Danae hoisted herself up by balancing on a large, heavy vase, "we entered via a lake and arrived on, well, not water. We don't even know where the entrance or exit to this place is."

Cassandra was stooped behind the counter. She emerged, moments later, with a scroll in hand. She shoved some vases aside and unrolled the papyrus. The other two hunched over her to get a look at the landmarks and cursive labels.

"When I got here, I landed in a field as well. Delphos is parallel to our world, but it's not a mirror per se. They seem to have switched around the locations of some things. Part of me wonders if it's framed after a cursed Greek city, like Atlantis, and that's why the topography is a little different."

True, the hill they climbed up felt more like a cliff, much like the topography in Greece. And the trees didn't resemble anything deciduous or evergreen someone would find in Ohio. More like spiky trees someone would find in the Mediterranean.

Good thing her Ancient History teacher made her do a group project on the topography of Greece. Who knew that would come in handy now?

"Lucky for you two, I've had thirteen years to sort all of this out."

Cassandra tapped a grove of illustrated trees with the label 'Semele.'

"Delphonians keep mentioning this is the place where the portal's gonna open. And from what I can tell, it's happening soon. Tonight, even. Mind you, it's not called Semele here."

Semele, the word sent her ears ringing. So she *had* noticed something different about that park. No wonder. Excitement buzzed in her veins.

The map rolled in Cassandra's fingertips, and she disappeared behind the counter again. This time, when she appeared, she had a leather pouch swung over her shoulder.

"In case something goes wrong or the portal takes longer than I thought, I brought provisions."

"Did you pack creamed corn too?"

Charity patted her back and felt naked with the absence of the Bowser book bag. If only she hadn't left it back at the lake. Think of how they could've put that Furbie to good use by now.

Wrinkles large enough to shelf vases formed on Cassandra's forehead. "Umm, no. That stuff's nasty. Even if you fed Krakkie that gunk, she'd probably retreat from Lake Prespa. Trust me. They eat snails in their diet here, and I still prefer those to creamed corn. Now," she stooped to collect the vases and return them to the shelves. The other two helped. "I don't know if any Delphonians are going to stake out the place, so it's important to put those good acting skills to use."

Danae and Charity shared a glance, and the former pursed her lips.

"She means you, Chair."

"I know, I know. Keep my head down, and no emotions."

"Or niceness." Danae jabbed a finger at her, inches away from her nose. "They're Delphonians. They kidnap little girls and turn people into sad gray monsters. Don't you go feeling sorry for them."

"Sorry."

Charity unwound the veil fabric from her wrist and re-placed the makeshift hood.

Once they finished returning the vases, Charity followed Cassie's sandals toward the entrance. Weak light peeked through. Even though they didn't have a sun here, or temperatures, she'd like to think they'd reached evening.

All the exciting zombie attacks happened at night.

Cassandra's sandals creaked when she reached the exit. She spun around and her fingers wove in and out of each other, like she was kneading dough.

"It's weird," Cassie's breath hitched, "saying goodbye."

"We could get captured and initiated," Danae pointed out.

"Yes." Cassandra clasped the side of the wall and leaned for support. "Wouldn't that be nice?"

Without another word, she spun around, and kicked up sand on the way out of the cloistered shops.

Keeping your neck bent down makes for a very boring journey in terms of scenery. Until we get to 'Semele' we'll carry out the next part of this section in a series of images.

Sand getting caught in Danae's shoes.

Grape juice spilling on someone's toga. Wait no, that smells way too strong to be grape juice . . . *sparkling* grape juice, obviously.

Legs. Lots of legs and feet. No touchy.

Basket full of apples.

Kid tipping over basket of apples.

Man tripping and slipping backward because of the basket of apples.

Long grass.

Blackberries clinging to the stalks of the long grass.

No wait, those are bugs.

Augh, augh, augh.

"We're here!"

By accident, Charity's neck snapped up, and she marveled at the black and white trees that stood in a circle around a cluster of Delphonians who had camped out. They were seated about fifty yards away, another race Charity's co-op made her do in elementary school. Spiky branches hugged one another in a conspiratorial fashion. A single pillar sloped on a hillside, like a slide that catapulted people off a cliff.

It was faint, but a single, blue light glowed on the hill. Charity couldn't get a clear enough look at the source without hoisting herself on her tiptoes. And any curiosity now could draw the band of Delphonians from under the trees.

Too bad the only splash of color here was mesmerizing. Memories from the park flashed in her mind. Didn't she spot a faint blue glow inside a slide covered in caution tape?

"Ugh." Cassandra slumped onto a nearby rock and brushed sand off her heels. "We're going to have to wait until all of them use the exit before we can get out. And who knows if they'll be waiting for us on the other side?"

Danae gulped. "There's a lot of them. Are they all going in at the same time?"

Charity imagined the portal getting clogged by the sheer amount of bodies. She tried to count them and reached thirteen before Cassandra chimed in and made her lose focus.

"I think they're sending in only a few of them to scout out the land. Heard your Zoan friend may be one of them."

Zoan?

Oh, she meant Io!

Charity tried to scan the crowd for her friend, but she couldn't make out the frizz-filled hair in the mess of gray limbs and bodies. "I don't see her." Anxiety pulsed in her fingertips. Would they leave this world without her friend? Danae hadn't made it clear how they'd get Io out of Delphos.

Buzzing filled her eardrums. An insect flitted past Charity and toward a grassy field.

A small Delphonian child lumbered after the black flying bug. Fascinating. Zombies came in fun size too.

"Can't we go at the same time as them?" Danae's voice stung Charity's ears as she continued to watch the kid. "Or even earlier. Like, now?"

"And risk getting touched? I'll take my chances. Plus it's hard to tell when that blue portal is going to be wide enough to fit a human. Cut your chances too close, and a part of you gets sliced."

No wonder they put caution tape on that slide. Did some kid get cut before they realized something funky had happened?

That could explain why the townsfolk got all quiet about Cassie and Delphos matters. Adults had a funny way of wanting to hush up anything weird or spooky.

"Well, then, doesn't that defeat the whole purpose of

keeping Delphonians out of Almsgiving?" Danae huffed. "We'd have to lure them back into the lake before closing the portal."

The child tripped on his one-size-too-large sandals and face-planted. Instinct took over, and Charity rushed toward him. His soft cries burned her ears. He must not have yet learned how to quell his emotions.

So did Delphonians learn the curse over time? Was the kid fighting the curse now? How did this all work?

She hovered over him and watched his small hands roll into fists and catch the blood from his nose. At least, it was dark liquid and most likely blood.

"Poor thi—"

"Charity," Danae barked, eyes wide. "What are you doing?"

Expression matching Danae's, Charity stiffened and turned her chin toward the grove of trees. A handful of Delphonians stared her down, in crouching stances. Like they either desperately needed directions for the restroom or were about to kick off for a race.

What? Oh! She backed away from the child in horror.

Oh no.

She fell backward and crashed onto a prickly patch of grass. Cassandra bolted toward her, Danae in tow. A single, high-pitched shriek sounded from the trees and then silence. And then the thunder of footsteps.

They were coming.

With a grunt, Charity stumbled into a stance and wobbled. Cassandra and Danae halted beside her as the Delphonians approached. They were now twenty yards away.

Cassandra dug into her pouch and several black olives rolled onto her palms. "Aim for between the eyes. It's a Delphonian weak spot."

Did the curse do that? Because if these people were human before, they must've gotten the weak spot afterward. Maybe like an Achilles heel, er, Achilles forehead.

Slimy briny-scented vegetables found their way into Charity's hands.

Oh yeah, time for a food fight.

She wound a pitch and aimed for a man with a large forehead. Thank the good Lord for basketball hoop shooting drills, because she smacked him right in the square on the backboard.

Danae beside her appeared to have similar luck. She wound three pitches and knocked out three women with the same style braid.

So they had cliques in Delphos as well.

Minutes later, the Delphonian troops had advanced five feet, and some decided they were smartypants and spread their reach wide until they'd formed a semicircle around the girls.

"We're running out of ammo." Cassandra dug into her satchel again. "And it won't be long before they close in. We need a new plan."

"New plan?" Danae missed the forehead of a Delphonian with a beard and pegged him in the eye instead. "Well, we can't outrun them, or out-olive them. Either we get initiated or we get through that portal."

"Too risky." Juice from Cassandra's fingertips formed puddles in the mud. "How'd you like to lose your left arm or spleen because they didn't fit?"

Seriously, how many injuries happened at that park before they put caution tape on that slide?

"Well, thanks to Miss Niceness over here, we don't have many options."

Guilt burned her stomach. Cassandra flung open the string on her back and with a sigh dropped the empty satchel onto the grass.

"Run."

They bolted around the enclosing circle of arms and hands and pathetic grunts and toward the hillside. The blue glow was about fifty yards away.

Danae and Cassandra bolted far in front of Charity.

Charity didn't dare look behind her, but based on the pounding of the Delphonian's footsteps, she imagined their arms could reach out and snag her at any second, the slowest runner of the group.

Fiery thorns wrapped around her lungs.

But she kept sprinting toward the edge of the hill.

Her breath hitched when they reached the pillar at last. Cassandra straddled one end like a horse saddle and peered at the blue light. Charity followed her gaze and her eyes magnetized to a blue, glowing ring that spun around at the column's end. Inside the circle was darkness. Nothing more.

It looked awful small at the bottom of that hill.

But Cassandra folded her hands and appeared to send up a quick prayer. Then she crossed her legs, laid back, and propelled herself down the column with her arms. She disappeared into the blue ring.

Seconds later, Danae followed. Pretzeled her legs, her arms, her heart, and hoped to live as she shot down the marble pole. Darkness consumed Danae.

Charity chewed on her lip and gazed at the revolving ring. The last two girls were skinny minnies. What would happen if the circle hadn't widened enough for her?

She glanced over her shoulder and her blood iced. Delphonians were mere yards away from the hillside.

Here went nothing.

With a slump, she straddled the column and peered into the shadowy band.

Please don't slice off my spleen, Mrs. Glowy Circle.

Footsteps rustled the grass overhead.

She crisscrossed her ankles, sucked in her gut, gave a hearty shove to the hill, and squeezed her eyelids shut.

Moments later, static electricity stung her hair. Too late, she thought. She hadn't passed through the portal alive.

Black greeted her when she opened her eyes, and then light beams glinted in the tunnel that smelled weirdly of plastic. Heaven needed to work on their transportation methods. She slid to the mouth of the burrow and squinted at a metallic monkey bar set covered in gray. A single crimson scar gleamed in the streetlight's beams. Beside it, Danae and

Cassie waited, arms crossed. Caution tape was still wrapped around Cassie's ankles.

Twisting around, she realized her hair stuck to the lip of the slide.

They'd returned to Semele Park.

Chapter 36

Should've Worn a Cooler Costume Before Dying. . . .

We don't have much time. Let's close that portal." Cassandra poked her head into the mouth of the slide while Charity attempted to smooth down the static in her hair.

"Great, let me just get my gallon of superglue." Danae rolled her eyes and gripped a rung on the monkey bars. "*The* book, with *the* incantation to close the portal is back at the lake. And last I checked, you didn't learn how to hotwire cars or even drive one in Delphos."

She signaled to the vehicles lined on the street.

"Did someone say, book?!"

A voice, male, shouted this. Silhouettes emerged from behind the plastic rock cave where Charity had found the spray-painted message, 'Find Alexandria.' That felt like a life-time ago.

Gray blanketed Hector's skin. He wore a gangster-style suit and hat, both pinstriped. The rest of the Delphonian gamers, several of which Charity spotted from their basement campaign, emerged into the wan streetlight. All bore a slate tint. Great, now that stupid librarian chick would kill her again, this time with her touch.

Legs shaky, Charity backed into a hard object. The monkey bars. No wonder Helen whacked her forehead on this mama. Whoever built this park decided to put this piece of playground equipment in the most inconvenient place possible.

Hector shot up a hand, and the group halted. "Guys, relax." He rubbed his thumb against the back of his hand until brown skin showed. "It's black and white makeup from my Al Capone Halloween costume."

Sure enough, everyone in the group showed splotches where they'd forgotten to blend the gray powder. Most, on the hand and neck areas.

"Figured we'd be here to close the portal, but also, to blend in—in case any invaders got through."

"Speaking of portals." Danae rushed over to the slide and banged her palm against the tube. The plastic made a 'thud' sound. "Why don't you stop talking and close this one? Like, now?"

True, when Charity had slid down the pillar, the Delphonians were yards away. Either they decided to quit and go for a game of pickleball, or they'd arrive any second.

"Two problems with that." Hector ticked off each one with a finger. "First, the incantation takes several minutes, and can't be interrupted. So if Delphonians started emerging and saw some dude in a snazzy suit trying to close the portal, they'd touch me, and game over."

Danae folded her arms. "And the second?"

A large wood chip buried under her sandal caused her to wobble. She caught her balance on the slide. Charity thought back to the child who had face planted in the field. How much his soft cries twisted knots in her stomach.

"Even if Hector closed the portal, he could kill Delphonians who were sliding down while he said the incantation. I know you don't like them, Danae, and I'm not exactly going to root for them in a thumb wrestling competition. But it would still be murder. They are, or at least, were humans at one point, right?"

Hector palmed the back of his neck. His other hand gripped the book by his side.

"Actually, I was going to say that there's a giant squid monster blocking the entrance at the lake, and we need to be able to close *both* the entrance and exit with the incantation. But the moral dilemma reason works too. Plus, we can't close it with the squid halfway on this side."

Cassandra tugged a curl away from her nose. "OK, so what *is* the plan?"

"Glad you asked. We hadn't accounted for you coming back, so we will have to modify the plan slightly. Also, a pleasure to meet your acquaintance, milady Cassandra. I'm assuming, you're Cassandra, right? Otherwise, it makes me wonder how many other people got kidnapped and taken into Delp—"

"Get to the point, Fedora the Explorer," Danae growled. "Zombies are going to pop out of that slide any second."

He cleared his throat.

"All righty. Myself, most-likely-Cassandra, Charity, and Miss Grumplestiltskin over here—"

Danae growled again.

"—are going to head to the lake. Thanks to Marian the Librarian borrowing her mom's fourteen-passenger homeschool van, we can escort the Delphonians to the lake using our clever disguises."

"Luckily, they're only sending a few spies to investigate the new world first before sending the whole army," Cassandra said.

Hector lifted the book in the air. "That's what this says too. Looks like we have some buffer time before a full-on invasion."

Charity clawed at a bug bite on her arm. How in the world was there a mosquito in Ohio in November? "Won't they find out you're Zoan?"

"We've had enough practice playing Hoplites. They can get into character long enough for a car ride to the lake."

The librarian clicked her keys. A car horn tooted from the street.

"As for those who stay behind, they'll wait for the Delphonians to get into the van and start the closing process. But it's up to us," he winked at Charity, "at the lake to find out a way to drive Mrs. Squid Monster back home."

He wriggled his fingers, imitating supernatural cephalopod tentacles.

"Once both portals are closed, everything should go

back to normal. No more infected people. No more curse. Any questions?"

"What about Io?" Charity interjected. Itchiness stung her eyeballs.

"Remember? I told you before the portal that she's with the spies. Helps to have a Zoan in their party who knows the land." Cassandra's expression softened. "Don't worry. We'll make sure your friend gets through. Even if we have to go through Krakkie again to get her."

Some oxygen left Charity's lungs from the breath she'd been holding. It wasn't a guarantee, but it was something. She'd have to trust Cassandra for now.

"All right, let's defeat a zombie army before school to-morrow." He slid his phone out of his pocket and glanced at the time. "Whoops, I mean later, this morning. Let's go."

With a wave, he motioned for Charity and the other Lake-goers to follow. They raced for the street and toward his car. She glanced down and groaned. Splotches, gray ones, had seeped onto her sandals. Why hadn't she realized the park was a portal to their world before?

She tugged open the door to the backseat and allowed for some crumpled napkins to spill onto the road before jumping in. Danae and Cassandra appeared to be having a near-silent bicker outside about who should take shotgun.

"I'm twenty-six years old. Oldest gets to sit in the front."

"It's by height, and let's be happy you can't drive. Bet you couldn't even reach the gas pedal."

"Ladies." Hector's voice wobbled in his throat. He rolled

down the window of the passenger seat. "Someone pick a seat. The invasion has begun."

Charity, who had chosen the back seat behind the driver, refrained from planting her palms on the fingerprint-laden window. She settled for a jaw sink instead.

Out the mouth of the slide trundled gray figures. Even from several feet away, she noticed how the light glinted off their wet lips.

She searched the figures for Io. Any minute now a zombie with frizzy hair would come somersaulting out . . .

. . . she hoped.

November mist swirled on the playground around every piece of equipment, except for the monkey bars.

A huff sounded behind her, followed by a door slam. Cassandra slid into the back seat and bunched her knees and arms. "You could at least move your seat up, you know."

Danae simpered and shoved her seat back another inch until Cassie's knees nearly knocked out her own teeth.

Hector dug the key into the ignition and the engine chugged to life. Part of Charity wished she could ask Hector to stay until she spotted Io.

Figures emerged from underneath the fake cave. Perhaps her imagination had played tricks on her, but she'd recognize the lanky figure of Stefan anywhere. Even in the dark.

But before she could get a better view, Hector slammed the gas. The haze of the park disappeared from her window in a blur of street lamps.

They sped toward a blinking yellow light.

The city turned off the red lights past a certain hour. No wonder, not a single active car seemed to exist on these skinny roads.

"Fedora, wanna walk us through how you managed to survive our friends getting initiated at the lake?" Danae gripped the cup holder, since the front seat didn't have an armrest. "How's your brother, by the way?"

The last part came out weak and thin, like she had choked on the words. Paris and Danae must've been closer than Charity thought.

"Dunno, haven't seen him. Everyone who got infected seemed to disappear. After I dodged the attacks and raced home, I returned a bit later that evening to see if there were any stragglers who would interfere with us trying to close the portal." He yanked the wheel to the right, and the car skidded. "No one was there. Maybe they went into the lake."

He shrugged, shoulders high enough to be seen from behind the seat. "So I sped-read the book—thanks to that handy dandy course I did at the library two summers back—formulated a plan, and used up the last of my black and white movie paint on the Hoplite gang."

Charity's eyes widened.

"Hector, you don't think—what would happen if we closed the portal on them?"

"We have to hope they *didn't* go in the lake."

Thirteen-sided dice plushies on the rearview mirror swung widely as they turned.

"You do have to keep in mind that the Delphonians want

out of Delphos," Cassandra pointed out. She sprawled her left leg so the seat couldn't squish it. "It's too overcrowded." Location, location, location. "Anyone initiated would probably stay put in Almsgiving, because their mind has been transformed into a Delphonian one."

Of course, *if* Almsgiving didn't disappear after all of the town got cursed.

Charity nodded, stomach tight, and stared at the embossed letters on the cover of the book. Hoped. Prayed. Then a horrible, icy realization hit her.

"What about our other friends? Like Stefan. He got touched." Charity's voice cracked.

Danae's shoulders slumped. Then rose. "One thing at a time. I'm sure when the curse gets reversed it could undo all the gray effects." She sniffed, perhaps from the cold weather. "Did anyone else escape Lake Prespa without getting touched? To warn people to stay indoors?"

"Sadly, no, but it is three o clock in the morning. The Delphonians picked a bad time to invade a town, when everyone's behind locked doors and asleep."

After a tense silence and five tire skids and turn signals later, they'd arrived at the school's parking lot.

"We don't have much time until the other group arrives." Hector unbuckled his seat belt. "Let's stakeout in the woods near the lake until the other group gets the Delphonian spies into the water."

"All except for Io, right?"

Everyone locked eyes onto Charity when she asked this.

Danae didn't speak for a moment. Then, "Of course. We'll tackle her to the ground if we have to. Just make sure to get your arms covered when we do that."

Hector swung open his door, and the group filtered out of the car.

"Better yet, we might want to split into two groups. In case the Delphonians catch on and start scouring the woods, we won't all be in one place, making it easy on them. Plus," he waggled his eyebrows at Cassandra, "I have so many questions about Delphos. Mind doing a Q and A, while we await possible death?"

Cassandra hmphed and hunched her shoulders. "Yes, that's the perfect way I want to spend my last night on earth."

Hector must not have caught on to the sarcastic tone, because he squeaked with giddy glee. Then, the two set off on the winding path toward the lake. Danae halted until they were halfway there before she marched onto the sidewalk.

The girls waited for Hector and Cassandra to take a heavily wooded section of the forest, and then they continued to the other end of the lake. A cold, heavy breeze almost knocked Charity onto her side. She hunched forward until they reached the edge of the trees. Although not-leafed, the trunks provided enough respite from the wind.

She slumped to the forest floor and grimaced when a root dug into her backside.

"Charity, if the Delphonians go rogue and come for the forest, I need you to promise me something." Danae clapped her spine against a tree and triangled her leg.

"I already know what you're going to say."

"Oh yeah?"

"'Put conditioner in your hair after you shampoo. And stop experimenting with the maple syrup in the shower.'" She stared at her hands. "'. . . and don't let my kindness or stupidity get in the way.'"

Even in the darkness, she could see the eye squinch from Danae.

Ohio had decided, for once, to give them a brilliant curtain of stars tonight instead of the usual fluffy cloud blanket.

Danae cleared her throat and fiddled with something on the ground. A stick. "I know you mean well, but meaning well has ended up getting several of our friends zombified, almost getting us initiated back in Delphos, and who knows what else?" She huffed. "Why are you so insistent on being nice? Especially to the Delphonians?"

"I don't know—"

Charity plucked a crunchy leaf and massaged the dead plant cell with her fingertips until plant dust filled her palm.

"—I guess, part of me wants to believe that there's good in everyone."

The breeze kicked up and spattered the leaf dust onto her toga. She thought back to Thanksgiving and the cranberry sauce. What had Mom told her before that incident?

"Your kindness always appears to perk people up."

"My mom, Stefan's, they seem like they're trying hard to fight the curse. They provided us rides when they didn't feel like it, and my mom even stood up for me at Thanksgiving."

244

Well, once. Gram-gram packed lots of punches.

Wind howled again, filling the forest with a wet, decayed-leaf scent.

Danae winced. "Even if they were fighting it, that was an earlier stage of the curse. By this point, they're probably fully initiated. Does your mom even care that you're missing tonight?"

Darkness clouded her chest.

Before she could put in a reply, voices stung her ears. She peered around her tree trunk and watched a group of Delphonians, led by the Librarian and another Hoplite player. Marian the Librarian flopped her arm in a lazy wave and kept her voice without color.

Sign that girl up for Broadway.

"As explained on the ride over here," she craned her neck toward the lake, "Oizys, leader of Delphos, recruited us ahead of time to scout this land for Delphonian safety. Tis habitable and suitable for population growth. You may report this pleasant news to the others and begin the invasion."

A Delphonian, one with a beard that went to his knees stumbled forward, kicking up sand. "Oizys, you said?"

Marian flinched, and even in the gray makeup, Charity swore she went two shades paler. She cleared her throat. "Why yes, Oizys. Who else could give such a command?"

Charity chewed on her lip and hoped Hector's speed-read, or whatever supplied Marian with this information, had been correct. Maybe it was from their campaigns. He did mention barbarians, though. Had he also introduced other anachronisms?

"Well," the Delphonian moved his arm to stroke his beard, but gave up on the effort after two seconds, "that was nice of you to scout everything and make our job easier." He glowered. "Don't do it again."

Right, Delphonians hated kindness. Also, apparently, they spoke English. Did they keep that skill with them when their town got cursed and Greek-i-fied? They must have. But this proved that Delphos originally started as an English-speaking town. And if they didn't act fast, Almsgiving would succumb to the same fate.

Charity counted the Delphonians at the lake. All ten of them. She kicked herself for not having numbered them back in Delphos. Then she could've known if Io made it back to Almsgiving.

Pretty sure there were more than ten, though.

Fear iced her arms and paralyzed them. What if Cassandra had heard wrong, and Io wasn't in the group of spies.

She let out a deep breath.

Trust for now. That's all you can do.

As the Delphonians continued to talk with the librarian at the lake, Charity thought back to the question she'd asked Cassandra. That did get them the information they needed. And back at Zoe's house too, and the snacks in Hector's front seat.

I've helped us piece together a lot of the clues.

Watery film stung her eyes. But this time, it wasn't from the Big Sad. More like a Big Happy.

If the curse ends, I helped in a big way.

Maybe she wasn't school smart. Or at least, after the Big Sad, it took her a while to get from Fs to Cs. But her Charity-smart helped to find Io and get back home with Cassandra.

Well, you couldn't have done it without Hector and all of them.

A warm sensation filled her chest. Maybe she didn't have to do this alone. All these years, trying to make the world a better place on her own. Maybe making the world a better place didn't have to rest on her toga-clad shoulders.

Or at least, she didn't have to battle a horde of zombies alone.

Now to work together to keep Io here, and end this stupid curse. It would take all of them, curses always seemed to work that way.

Conversation fizzled. The spies staggered into the lake. Panic squeezed Charity's chest. She didn't spot Io amongst them, but did she count them right? What if they demoted Io from the spies at the last minute?

Splashes disappeared moments later when one by one they plunked underwater. Krakkie got a fun midnight snack.

Tension released in her abdomen, and she craned her neck back at Danae.

"Coast's clear as a—"

She froze. No time to finish that simile, which may or may not have included an axolotl and a sprocket. A cloaked figure in a toga reached an arm around the tree, gray fingers inches away from Danae's shoulder blade. Danae was fixated on the lake.

Instinct kicked in and three things happened at the same time.

One: Charity either shouted "No!" Or "Ugh, what a kill-joy." Or both at the same time. Everything happened so fast, she couldn't keep track of what words got shouted.

Two: Charity dove in front of Danae, barricading the attacker from touching Danae's exposed skin.

Three: Charity's makeshift hood had long since whipped off in the wind.

So the cold fingertips landed on her neck instead.

Chapter 37

Should've Known, Even Creamed Corn Has Its Uses. . . .

Blue light exploded in the forest.

If this was what going to heaven felt like, Charity didn't like it. Her neck seared, and judging by the pained howl from the cloaked figure, they weren't having the time of their lives.

Her heartbeat throbbed in her neck, and she crumpled to the floor. Wet leaves dabbed her knees. Through slit eyelids, she watched the neon beams crawl up the hooded figure's arm. The glow showed underneath the toga until the flare illuminated the figure's entire body.

Then, sudden darkness fell over the forest.

With a groan, the figure threw off their hood. Charity, still squinting from the subsiding neck throb, had to wait several seconds for her eyes to adjust. Luckily, her ears were still working.

"Ugh, my head. Please don't do

that again."

A grin threatened to slice Charity's cheeks. "Io!"

By now, her eyes had adapted to the dark lighting, and she noticed the gray splotches had disappeared from Io's arms. Was she . . . ?

Either way, no harm in risking a hug.

Charity shook as she stood and then barreled into Io. She squeezed so tight that Io had to tap her on the back when she needed to breathe again. Still, she made sure not to touch skin when they hugged . . . in case.

When they staggered back, a headache throbbed in Charity's temples.

Yikes, sacrificing yourself did come with physical repercussions.

Tears squeezed out of Charity's eyelids. This time, she allowed them to fall and didn't blame them on any lake gastric conditions.

She'd cried many times after Io had left them. Maybe it was OK to acknowledge the Big Sad from time to time. As long as she did what she could to fight it. Like her mom.

"Y-you," Danae's voice shook behind her, "you didn't turn into a . . . how?"

They both glanced expectantly at Io, who was busy massaging her forehead. "Look, I just came back to life, I don't have many answers." She winced. "But, from what I can remember when I had a Delphonian mind—hazy memories, mind you—they hate kindness."

She crumpled to her knees and rolled her head into her

250

stomach like a sushi. Pains stabbed Charity's skull with each heartbeat. If this was how they would save the rest of their initiated friends, she didn't know if she could do it.

Dark splotches filled her vision. But again, it *was* really dark in this forest.

Io untucked her head. "Something about Charity diving in to save you must've made the curse rebound. Like it's allergic to kindness or something."

Shoulder first, Danae fwumped into a tree. She leaned and chewed on her bottom lip. "So . . . us doing kind things actually could've helped fight the curse?" Her voice came out quiet, not a whisper, but definitely not the usual strong Danae timbre.

"Don't go too hard on yourself." Io squinched her eyelids. "From what I can remember from what I heard from the scouting group—again, *really* hazy memories—because the Delphonians hate altruism, the curse latched onto the kindest people in the vicinity to be its carriers."

That they knew.

"Especially thirteen-year-olds, because the first girl to get cursed was thirteen."

That, they . . . sort of knew?

"So part of the curse made your kind acts have disastrous consequences, so you'd not want to do them. When the Delphonians invaded, you'd sit back and do nothing."

Now, they didn't know *that*.

Danae picked at the bottom of her torn toga. "So you were with the Delphonian spies. Thought I spotted you." She

251

tapped the bridge between her nose. "Sorry if I pegged you with an olive."

Io grinned and brushed the space between her eyebrows with her fingertips.

"Speaking of spies," Danae pushed herself off the tree, "how'd you spot us? No one else going into the lake even looked back our way. And," she threw up her hands, "you don't need to tell us if the memory was too hazy."

With a sudden grimace, like she'd been force-fed creamed corn, Io's eyes darted in horror to the other end of the forest.

"It wasn't *you* who I spotted first."

"Then who—?"

Grunts cut off Danae's question. Two silhouettes ahead staggered toward them. One large, the other, very short.

"You initiated Cassandra and Hector?" With a quick arm-jerk, Danae motioned for them to follow. Then she sprinted toward the lake.

"In my defense, it was the Delphonian in me. I, she . . . I don't know, whoever! They spotted two figures hiding in the trees. I, she—"

Io pinched the bridge of her nose as she ran beside Charity.

"We'll call her Janis, OK? Janis snuck to the edge of the woods, and I remember the two Zoans were distracted. He was asking her questions or something. So I reached from behind the tree and initiated him, and I guess the big guy was hard for the woman to dodge around, so he passed it onto her."

They halted near the shore. Icy water lapped over Charity's feet. The two from the homeschool van had disappeared. Maybe they went back to the park or, like Hector, needed to be motivated by snack payments, and decided they were one Twinkie short from their obligation to save the world.

"That doesn't make any sense." Danae stooped and picked up some chunks of driftwood. "Cassandra lived in Delphos for thirteen years. You mean, all it took was a guy in a fedora to do her in?"

"Ask Janis, OK? I'm only remembering bits and pieces, when I was trying to fight it."

Memories from Thanksgiving flooded Charity's mind. So her mom *had* tried to battle the curse. Hope lit a fire in her chest.

The warmth died moments later when the now-gray Hector and Cassandra emerged from the columns of trees. (Well, yes, Hector was technically in black and white make-up, so that would make him gray to start with. But the drool that glistened on his lips sort of was a dead giveaway . . . or really an *undead* giveaway. Hahahahaha, OK, sorry). Charity scanned the sand for more driftwood.

Music from the Pyscho theme stung her ears. Now crumpled on her knees, she craned her neck forty-five degrees and landed on a lumpy object.

Wait a moment. She spotted white fabric spikes. Her Bowser backpack!

She crawled over, kicking up sand, and dove for the large

zipper. Out slid her cell phone. An unknown number blared on the screen. She slid open the green call button.

"Hello! Charity speaking, how may I assist you before I lose all my memories and the ones I hold dearly?"

"You the kid who filled in for me as a mystic and got my character killed?" A sharp voice on the receiver caused her eardrum to throb.

Oh, oh no . . . .

Delphonians come initiate me now before I get killed by this chick.

Charity swallowed. "Umm, yes?"

"Well, thanks. I've been looking for an excuse to do the speech and debate team competitions on Saturdays. Figured I'd break Hector's heart if I just up and left. I even made up the part about the concussion. So anyway, how are things on your end?"

Danae chucked a piece of wood at Hector. The chunk rebounded off his large forehead.

"Oh, dandy."

"Any luck in getting the Kraken away from the entrance? We can't close both portals until they're free of blockage."

Her eyes flicked to the dark lake. Then to the two girls hurling driftwood. Their woodpile had been reduced to five slabs. They'd run out of ammo soon.

"Yeah . . . about that."

"Charity, we need you to get that portal unblocked. The spies went into the lake a few minutes ago, and we don't know how long until the invasion's going to start. I've already had to call back up here because there's some initiated Delphonians circling in on us."

So that's where the homeschool van folks went.

"Initiated Delphonians?"

"Yeah, one looks like Hector's brother."

Her veins froze. That's where Paris and Stefan and everyone else who got infected must've gone, to the park. She *knew* she spotted Stefan from the van when Hector had hit the gas.

"Hurry!"

The line went dead. Io chucked her last piece of drift-wood. She missed his body entirely by two inches.

"Don't ever sign up for softball," Danae grumbled.

"It's dark out. And the best you did was nail someone on the forehead. *Not* in-between the eyes."

"Any chances you could just throw yourself at them, like Charity did back for you in the forest?"

"I don't know what'll happen if two of them reach for you at once. No telling if the curse will rebound on both of them. It's too risky. Plus," Io panted, "it's exhausting and hurts."

Charity dug her fists into the sand to find something else solid they could throw when her eyes landed on the Bowser backpack.

Contents from earlier, what Stefan had packed for her, were strewn next to the bag in the sand. She slapped on the Ninja turtles mask and propeller hat, like battle armor.

She scooped the Furbie and the expired cinnamon roll

tube. The latter oozed a sticky residue onto her fingertips. "Io, Danae, catch!" She tossed the two items at them, and the fwump that followed seconds later indicated that they let them drop into the sand. Returning to the items by the backpack, she gripped their last hope.

Creamed corn.

A sharp breath puffed out her nostrils. Here was to hoping Krakkie had a refined palette.

With a groan, she drew her arm back and thrust the can toward the waters.

Plunk.

Moonlight glinted on the aluminum lid for the briefest moment before the vessel disappeared into the depths.

Whack. She turned and watched Danae wallop Hector between the eyes with the cinnamon roll canister. His knees slammed the sand, and he howled. Moments later, Io managed to pitch a miracle Furbie line drive. Cassandra slumped.

Neon blue lights stunned her peripherals, and she twisted back to the lake. A large distorted ring glowed underneath the waters. One Mississippi, two Miss—the glow died.

Krakkie must've retreated when she tasted the creamed corn.

"Ugh, that's the last time I'm ever doing a Q and A with a fanboy."

Charity whipped around to find Cassandra massaging her forehead. Her heart skipped and she raced over to give a hug. Halted. Drew her fingers together. What if . . . .

Cassandra's lips twitched, and she removed her fingers

from her skull and clasped Charity's hand. Charity flinched. Cold, cold fingers. Then she relaxed.

"It's gone. The curse is gone."

Pro tip for after saving the world: Take off the Ninja turtles mask. Otherwise your tears get caught on the bottom of the plastic chin.

She tore the mask off and flung her arms around Cassandra. Bodies piled around her for a warm group hug. Even though the November breeze kicked up at their legs, she couldn't feel the cold.

Io and Charity looped arms together, and Charity couldn't contain the amount of sunlight within her. She felt as though the beams could practically burst out of her chest and blind all of them.

At last, she'd gotten Io back, Cassandra un-kidnapped . . . and there was the matter of Stefan back at the park. He must've gotten the curse reversed too.

They released, and Danae swiped at a tear that had burned down her cheek. "How'd the Krakken get out of the entrance?"

"Turns out, even squids don't like creamed corn."

Danae's lip sagged. "How'd the portal not chop off any tentacles? We didn't see a blue glow until Krakkie disappeared. So her head must've been large and should've been sliced when she entered our lake."

"She's built like an octopus," Cassandra pointed out. "They can squeeze their bodies into tight spaces. Her head must've ballooned after she entered the portal, the rest of her body constricted so it could fit in the hole. And besides, she's a supernatural cephalopod that eats dead skin cells. It's best not to question particulars."

Fair.

Hector dug into his pocket and his keys jangled. "Let's get you all home."

Cassandra slumped, if that was even possible given her height, and banded her waist with her arms. "I doubt I could go back to my childhood home." She gazed at the lake, eyebrows furrowed. "Maybe I should've stayed behind."

Charity elbowed her playfully in the ribs. "We have a couch in our basement that's covered in stuffed animals my mom has won at the county fair . . . just kidding, she bought them all for ten dollars apiece at Wal-Mart and tells everyone she won them at the bottle toss."

She grinned and angled toward the windy path. "It's calling your name."

Chapter 38

Should've Created a Chart About the Hierarchy of Hugs. . . .

Her mom looked so peaceful asleep. Skin, in the shafts of yard lights from outside the window, no longer ashen.

Charity jabbed a finger in the air and glowered at it. Like reverse Sleeping Beauty and that poisonous spindle.

To poke or not to poke?

It probably would be rude to jab her mom in the cheek and wake her at this hour. But pre-cursed Mom did like to work out on the basement treadmill in the mornings. Something told her that her mother wouldn't appreciate finding a random woman snuggling with the stuffed elephant.

The finger crashed against her mother's cheek.

Mom stirred and peered at Charity through slits. She moaned. "Mmm wha-is it?"

"I'm having a friend stay the night. Is that OK?"

Crack went Mom's back when she

stretched her arms toward a wooden headboard. "Mmm, sure swee-har—"

"We're going to get her set up on social media to find her parents. They were against her getting it when she was a teen, but I figure since she's twenty-six, that they may let this one slide."

"Mm."

"She wants to head into the police station tomorrow, too, to show them that she's alive. I told her we have to drive to school first, and she seems chill about it. 'Education comes before revealing to the law enforcement that you're not dead.'"

Big yawn. "Sounds goo—" Her mother's head clapped against the fluffy pillow. Yeah, she was definitely not awake.

Tip for revealing that you're letting a missing twenty-six-year-old stay in your basement: Ask the parents at two in the morning.

Charity eyed the clock on the side table. 2:04. She'd have to sneak some coffee in four hours to get through the school day tomorrow. That or the secret stash of hardened jelly beans from her Easter basket.

She'd decide which when her alarm went off at 6:15.

With a lip twitch, Charity squeezed her mom's hands and let the electricity run through her fingertips. No longer cursed.

It was a wonderful feeling.

Sheets rustled when she slipped off the bed and toward the door. She paused when she reached the knob and craned her neck back to her mother. Mom had already face-planted into the pillow.

"Thanks, Mom."

"For wha-sweehar-?"

She clicked the knob and slipped into the hallway. When she pressed the door shut, she placed her ear and arm against the grooves. Almost like she was giving the entryway a hug. She'd get plenty of practice doing the different types of hugs at school tomorrow . . . more importantly and highest in the hierarchy of embraces: the bear hug.

Pat, pat. She tapped the door twice with her palm. "Thanks for fighting so hard against the curse." A tear burned down her cheek. "We won."

Epilogue

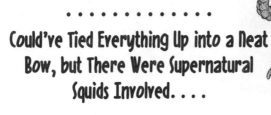

Could've Tied Everything Up into a Neat Bow, but There Were Supernatural Squids Involved. . . .

I don't know about this, Danae."

"Get in the water, Fedora. All the other Delphonian Hoplite players did the initiation."

Hector did not, in fact, wear a fedora today.

Instead, clad in a toga, he shivered on the red plastic steps that led up to the hot tub. All the other Hoplite players, who had already taken a plunge, watched from behind glass windows, all now in warm sweaters and sweatpants.

He drew the folds of his toga tighter into his chest and stepped into the steam-filled pool. Then he spun around and plugged his nose. Deep breath, he plunged into the tub. Jets spit rushes of white water, and the underwater lights changed colors from yellow to blue.

When he broke the surface, those surrounding the tub in togas clapped.

"Welcome to the Cassandra Coalition." Danae motioned for Paris to grab a towel off a nearby wooden patio chair. "Of course, as none of us are cursed any longer, the Coalition is now open to anyone who wants to spread kindness in small ways."

Charity, huddled between two Coalition members, grinned and stared at the clouds. Never had a gray sky looked so beautiful than on this Saturday.

"OK, everyone, hot tub time, and then we'll get ready to head our service project of the week. Who's up for making quilts for homeless women?"

A trembling Hector exited the hot tub and grabbed the towel from Paris. The rest of the toga-clad kids charged up the steps and into the tub. Thirteen initiations took far longer than one would think, especially whilst shivering in the Mid-December cold.

When enough bodies had piled into the tub, leaving the water brimming over the edges, Charity gathered the train of her toga, which dragged on the wet patio pavement, and headed indoors.

Heat warmed her arms and calves when she entered. She spotted a soaked Stefan by the snack table. His hair had glued down to his forehead, shielding some of the acne.

She slid onto the chair beside him and poked black olives onto all her fingertips until her hand looked like a gecko's. Thumb in her mouth, she made one olive disappear and left behind a briny, wrinkled finger.

"Didn't feel like getting in the hot tub either?" she asked.

"Figured it didn't make sense for me to get in, get initiated, get out, get changed, get back in, and then what? I'd have no more clothes to wear. Have to put on your dinosaur onesie before sewing quilts with old ladies."

Charity snickered and chewed on another olive.

Stefan reached for a cheeseboard with cheddar and crackers. "Although I am happy that Danae changed the purpose of the Coalition. We can do a lot of good to a lot of people who feel cursed."

"Speaking of," Charity swallowed, "what was it like? Being under the spell?" She wriggled her fingers.

"I mean, I'm sure Io's told you a lot of the details are fuzzy—"

Io was in a large chair in the family room, chatting with Marian the Librarian about holiday traditions. She had a plastic plate full of frosted cookies balanced on her knee.

"—but I do remember it was really hard to fight. The thing made you feel empty of all feeling, emotions. You sorta stumbled around and did the bare minimum. Like, even if the curse didn't take thirteen years to open up the portal in Semele, I have a feeling it would've taken that long for the Delphonians to get organized and invade."

Charity bobbled her chin and stared at a celery stick that had collapsed onto the carpet in a splotch of ranch.

"You know, Stef, I was really worried you wouldn't want to be friends, especially after I grabbed your ankle at the lake. So many of the Coalition members had friends leave them even after minor effects of the curse, let alone getting initiated."

"Are you kidding?" Stefan popped a sliver of cheese onto

his tongue. "My best friend turned me into a zombie. How cool is that? Best Christmas gift ever."

A wry smile wriggled up Charity's cheeks. She turned her gaze back to the family room and her eyes caught on the blue crystal star placed on the hilt of the Christmas tree.

Sapphire ribbons and fairy lights chased each other down the spiraled branches.

Already got the best Christmas gift this year, maybe even this lifetime: I can hug anyone who barrels into my way.

"Still," Stefan pulled her from her thoughts and bit into a cracker, "I'm glad Mom's back to normal. I'm starting to think peanut butter and pickles don't work all that well on sandwiches. Also, Dad took his loss pretty poorly in the tennis tournament. Apparently, Paris' dad took him out with goose-egg sets. Brutal."

A doorbell chime interrupted the last word. She flicked her gaze to outside, where Paris and Hector flung water at each other in the tub.

Well, someone might as well answer.

With a groan, her chair scooted back. She raced to the door and clicked the knob.

"Cassandra!"

"Hey there, nice toga." She winked. Charity gave a spin in her dinosaur-printed sheet outfit. Unlike some lame-os like Stefan, she *would* wear this to the quilting event later. "Thought I'd stop by to say goodbye. Thanks for getting me re-set up on social media. It's certainly changed a lot in thirteen years."

Two days into searching, Cassandra at last found her mom, who had a different last name and lived in a different state. Minnesota.

They chatted, shared many tearful video chats, and after being questioned to death by the local law enforcement, Cassandra had decided she'd get home for the holidays before any more newspapers could slap her photo and the word "Found" onto the front cover.

"Figured I have thirteen Hanukahs to catch up on." Her gaze hovered over the presents underneath the tree. Paris and Hector's parents apparently enjoyed silver, shiny wrapping, and ramen-noodle-shaped bows. "Thanks for suggesting I meet up with Zoe." She swallowed and swayed back and forth. "It was tough, but worth it."

After Io and Cassandra had collaborated beforehand on what story they'd tell the police—

The fake story they told the police: We were kidnapped by a man with the last name of Delphos. He always wore a ski mask, so we never got a good look at him. His skin was gray.

—after all, this story wouldn't have worked—

The real story: So yeah, uh, we were taken to a parallel world in a lake via a supernatural squid. And Cassie here spent several years blending into a zombified culture until, thirteen years later, a portal to her exit emerged on a pillar that led into a slide in a local park. No, we're not crazy. Why do you ask?

—anyway, Charity suggested Cassandra go talk with Helen's remaining relative in town. Anytime their car flew past Semele Park, tears would stain Cassandra's cheeks. After a lot of pushback, and some bribes that may have involved getting ice cream at The Scoop, Cassandra paid Zoe a visit.

"She was mad at first, but after we talked over bubble tea, she took me to Helen's grave. It's really pretty. Someone puts Asphodelian flowers there every week. Little white flowers with six petals. Zoe has no idea who."

Cassandra leaned against the door and rubbed her fingers on the wreath. The bristles made a scratchy sound.

"I've done a lot of damage, kid. After I catch up with Mom, I'm going to have quite a few wounds to stitch up. And I'm going to have a lot of bad Delphonian habits to unlearn. Something tells me I won't be in Minnesota for long."

She blinked away a glaze and cleared her throat.

"Anyway, I suppose this is goodbye for no—oof!"

Charity barreled into her in a bear hug, and they almost slid off the front stoop. Lucky for them, Cassandra grabbed hold of a porch pillar. After two Mississippis, they released.

"Miss you too, kid." Cassandra winked and stuffed her fists into her coat pockets. She turned and ventured down the driveway.

At the base, smoke exhaust puffed from a car. When Charity squinted, she spotted Zoe in the driver's seat.

Gusts stung her cheeks and she backpedaled indoors and slammed the front door. She flinched when she noticed another body right next to hers. Io was busy inspecting the shoes.

"Charity, did you bring your sandals today?"

"What else was I supposed to wear with my toga," she

snorted, "my dinosaur slippers?"

"Which ones are they?"

"Look for the shoes with the sparkly pink poking out underneath brown paint."

After a close inspection of the massive pile of shoes by the front door, Io managed to locate the pair. She slit her eyelids as she surveyed the footwear up and down.

"You'd mentioned they turned gray at the park, but you noticed they went back to brown when you got home."

Other Delphonian Hoplite players had reported various garments had turned to gray, mostly shoes since they already brought gray sheets to the park in the first place.

But by school the next day, word passed around that everyone's clothes that had touched the park's surface had gone back to their original shade. Thus, the curse had yielded its grip on every town object.

"Yeah, why?"

Io dug into the pocket of her sweats underneath her toga and pulled out the thirteen-sided die. Charity had given it to her in the ride back home. A souvenir to remember everything.

Although the die had appeared red that night, it was unmistakably gray in Io's palm now.

"Why do you think it turned back to gray?" Io's voice quivered.

Ice filled Charity's veins for the briefest of moments. But when her gaze rested on the pink sparkles underneath the thin-brown paint on her sandals, her shoulders relaxed.

"It could be a prank. Maybe Hector managed to grab the die when you weren't looking and painted it." Here was to hoping Hector used thicker paint than she had on the sandals. "Or replaced it with one of his own gray die to scare you."

She hoped. Based on how much Io's shoulders dropped, it looked like her friend was hoping too.

"You're right," a nervous chuckle bounced in Io's throat. "That's gotta be it." She shivered. "Bit cold by the front door, don't you think?"

A draft pricked her neck. She thought back to the forest when Io's cold fingers crashed onto her skin.

"Yeah, let's go back to the family room." They turned and headed toward the room with the crackling fire. She loved the sound the wood made when the embers popped.

Some Coalition member, wrapped in a hoodie, had stolen Io's seat.

They stationed themselves by the fire, and Charity watched the flames dance in Io's pupils.

"You know, Chair," Io propped her elbows on the stone landing by the fireplace and rested her chin on her knuckles, "what you did back in Delphos, when you went to help that boy who had fallen, was—"

"Stupid." Her cheeks burned.

"—incredible."

Stunned, Charity blinked. The heat from the fire had dried out her eyes.

"Listen, I wasn't initiated for long. Time moves and feels differently in Delphos. But everything we've been told about

Delphonians may not be entirely correct."

Io traced indiscernible shapes into the thick carpet. She paused and stared at a swan ornament that dangled from the bottom Christmas tree branches.

"When I was first taken to Delphos, before Cassandra accidentally initiated me, I tried to blend in with my surroundings. Everyone kept their heads hunched, so I played along."

Pop, sizzle, crack went the fireplace.

Charity drew her knees to her chin and listened, absorbing all of Io's words.

"When I arrived, a Delphonian woman, one of the spies, took me into her home. Offered food, a really hard mattress to sleep on. Granted, she did do it while glaring at me and grumbling the whole time, but the whole hospitality thing surprised me."

She sketched a circle into the carpet with her fingers.

"After all, Delphonians hate kindness. But maybe there's something to Delphos that we're missing. Sure, they're sad and detached. But if they offered me a home and they trained Cassandra how to do pottery, there's gotta be more to them than what's in that book."

The circle stopped.

Even though lively conversations continued at the snack table behind them, and laughter rang from the outside door as the hot tub goers stumbled inside, dripping onto the hardwood, Charity felt as though a hush had fallen over the family room.

"Ah well." Io shrugged and rolled the die onto the carpet. It landed on number thirteen. "The portal's closed, so I guess we don't have to worry about these questions, huh?"

Charity glanced back at the group. Paris was busy making scissor hand gestures about how he'd cut fun shapes into his quilt. Danae giggled beside him and leaned in closer. She turned back to the die and squinted at its gray shade for an inhale and exhale.

Inhale, one Mississippi.

Exhale, two Mississippi.

Charity winced. "Yeah, haha, I guess we couldn't care less."

Acknowledgments

Should've Never Written Something This Silly in the First Place....

But since I did, I have the following people to blame.

To my Lord and Savior Jesus Christ. Humans all appear to have a Cassandra Curse of some sort.

We are not kind to one another. We may not dress up in clown costumes and give peanut treats to those who undergo anaphylactic shock (at least, I should hope not), but we can use a great deal more kindness and empathy in the world. Thank you for leading the example and through your kindness, giving yourself up for us.

To Tessa Emily Hall and Cyle Young. You poor agents who have to sneak this book into the inboxes of editors. What a weird bequeathment I have placed at your disposal. Thank you for bearing with my craziness and numerous emails. I know how hard it is to get a project in front of the right eyes, and am so thankful for the hours you have invested in me.

To Alyssa, Sonya, Carlee, and James. My goodness, you all are dangerous encouragers. Get a load of these guys. The minute I want to give up, they bombard me with memes and uplifting notes and all sorts of gross stuff like that.

You ridiculous narwhals. Let me quit, you fools.

To my family who has expanded a great deal over the years. Whether we are related by blood or by water or some other cool liquid (just not lake water, please) you have encouraged me so much on this journey. You have shared my social media posts an embarrassingly high number of times and supported me the whole way through.

To the professional writing department at Taylor University who originally gave me a writing prompt that involved me creating a character who, though she meant well, wreaked disaster any time she did something kind. I knew, from having written that short story, that I wanted to explore Charity a little more. Especially to the Cyle Henchfolks, thanks for letting me post random stuff in the chat and for not booting me out.

To my cat who sits next to me on the couch as I write this and looks very annoyed. He claims I have not fed him in 6.7 years. Don't listen to him. It was 6.5.

And of course, to my really weird readers who for some reason have found themselves in the acknowledgments section. Are you lost? Do you need to use a GPS? Well, now that I've trapped you here, I want to thank you for reading this wacky tale.

Always be kind, and together, we can make all schools allow for dinosaur onesies to be part of their dress codes. The only true hidden agenda in this book. You've caught me.

Now let's make it happen.

About The Author

Hope Bolinger

Hope Bolinger is a nerd, and worse, a hardworking nerd, the most devious of combos. She's an editor at Crosswalk.com and a graduate of Taylor University's professional writing program. More than 1,200 of her works have been featured in various publications ranging from Writer's Digest to Keys for Kids. She has worked for various publishing companies, magazines, newspapers, and literary agencies and has edited the work of bestselling authors.

Fourteen of her books are out or under contract, with *Cassandra Curse* being her first endeavor into the weird world of middle grade. When she isn't going crazy and writing a novel in nine days, you can find her in her downtown dressed up in a costume for no reason. Find out more about her at her website: hopebolinger.com

Chicken Scratch Reading School

The Cassandra Curse – Novel Study Course

www.chickenscratchbooks.com/courses

Join us at Chicken Scratch Reading School for an online Novel Study Course for *The Cassandra Curse*. Created by certified teachers with extensive curriculum design experience, this offering is a full 6-week course of study for 5th-8th grade students. It includes reading study focus, quizzes, vocabulary work, thematic and writing device analysis, a written essay, and culmination project. The course includes a mix of online and on-paper work, highlighted by instructional videos from the author, Hope Bolinger, and publisher Kiri Jorgensen.

Chicken Scratch Books creates online novel study courses for every book we publish.

Our goal is to teach our readers to appreciate strong new traditional literature.

At Chicken Scratch Books,
Traditional Literature is all we do.

We Fill the Gap

Mainstream Publishers

Religious Publishers

Mainstream and Religious
Children's Book Publishers
used to run side-by-side.

Now they've split